WAYWARD GUARDIAN

Book 1 of the Guardian Saga

BY: ARLIN FEHR

Wayward Guardian

CHARACTERS

Howard Fredrick: Captain

Sophie Fredrick: Howard's Wife

Mark Jona: First Mate

Keith Loheim: Chief Engineer

Ira Geer: Nurse

Ayla Geer: Ira's daughter

Samuel Jennings: Ship's Advocate

EXO: Ships AI Guardian Core

James Bennet: Colonial Power Grid Overseer

Danny Hough: Chief of Security

Sarah Lough: Hydroponics Technician

PROLOUGE

REASONS

Howard and Sohpie's Home

Another message from Axion waited for him. Howard didn't even bother opening it. Again and again, they had tried to get him to be the captain for a new colonial mission. Again and again, he'd turned them down.

'What's wrong Howard?' asked his wife, Sophie, looking over his shoulder.

'Axion again. They won't relent.'

Howard set his datapad down on the table and reached behind him, pulling one of her hands onto his shoulder. He gave it a squeeze, and she squeezed back.

'They must want the best man for the job,' she said.

'I'm not the only man for the job though.'

'No, but you've got a lot of experience under your belt.'

Howard turned in his chair. The dining room was bright with sunshine, and their quaint country home beamed with warmth.

He looked at his wife and realised how much more frail she looked. It was especially noticeable this spring, as though the winter had sapped more of what little remained of her life.

'I've been gone enough,' he told her gently.

She shuffled over to one of the other chairs, Howard made to get up and help her, but she waved him back down.

With a lump in his throat, he watched her slowly take a seat, the effort clear on her face.

Once she was settled, Howard relaxed a little and watched her. She had something on her mind, he could tell that much. Something he didn't want to say.

Outside the window, a bird lighted on their apple tree and chirped. Howard looked at it with a mix of contentment and bitterness. How many such moments had he already missed with his wife because he'd been gone to space so much already.

'I know what you're thinking Howard,' Sophie said.

He looked at her and smiled sadly. 'What am I thinking my dear?'

'You're thinking that you wished you hadn't been gone so much. I saw the way you looked at that bird.'

Howard nodded. 'You're right my dear.'

She raised a finger towards him and shook it slowly. 'Don't think like that Howard Friedrick. If it wasn't for your times out there as a ship captain, I never would have lived as long as I have. Treating me hasn't been cheap you know.'

Howard leaned his head back and sighed. 'I know that. I'm still not happy about it.'

'I've had a good life you know.'

5

Howard shook his head. 'Don't talk like that, you aren't dead yet.'

Her face flashed with frustration. 'I know that. I don't plan on changing that fact any time soon either.

'Sixty-six years old, and you still don't know how to talk to your wife,' she said.

'I'm still figuring it out. It's an ongoing project,' he replied.

She nodded.

They sat there in silence for what seemed like a long time, just living the moment together. Finally, Sophie broke the silence.

'I think you should accept Axion's offer.'

Howard frowned, feeling a twinge of anger.

'What? How can you say that?' he asked.

Sophie looked equally frustrated at his reaction. 'It's not such a bad idea. The offer is a great one, and we both know that I'm going to need more attention. Our insurance won't cover everything on its own, but Axion will. They know the situation. They offered it themselves. I read the offer last time you showed it to me.'

Howard raised a hand, ready to say something, but couldn't find the words. Slowly he lowered his hand down.

After a moment, he said, 'I don't want to be gone anymore.'

'Doctor Patel has an experimental treatment he wants to try, something cutting edge, but because it's not a mainstream treatment, our insurance won't cover it,' she said.

'What? When did you find this out?'

'Just this morning. I... didn't know how to tell you. I didn't want to get your hopes up.'

Howard couldn't help but smile. 'I appreciate that, unfortunately, it didn't work. My hopes are up.'

'You could take the mission and come back home when it's over,' she offered.

Howard nodded, 'I could. What if it doesn't work though? Then that's more time we don't have.'

Sophie smiled. 'But we'd have a chance at more time together.'

'Alright. I'll send them a message.'

***

Howard sat at his home computer, a much more comfortable place to have a discussion than with his tablet at the table. Sophie was seated in the room too, out of view of the camera but well within earshot.

'Axion Data Sytems, Landon Richards speaking.'

'Landon, it's Howard Fredrick speaking.'

'Captain Fredrick!' the face on the screen smiled at him warmly, 'I hope this means you've reconsidered our offer.'

Howard nodded quickly. 'I have actually. I've decided to accept.'

'That's wonderful news! I can send you the documenta-'

'However, I do have some conditions.'

Landon's face shifted into a more serious and focused expression. 'That's fine, let's talk conditions then. Axion is very eager to have a man of your experience leading this mission.'

'Glad you're willing to hear me out. Firstly, I will need to be paid half my mission compensation now, and half upon completion of the mission.'

Landon leaned back in his seat. 'That is an unusual request given what I've read about your employment history, you don't usually work that way.'

'I have certain obligations that I have to meet before I can leave Earth again, I'm sure you understand,' Howard said.

Landon nodded. 'I'm sure we can work with that. Anything else?'

'I need my wife to be covered under the Axion Medical plan, despite a preexisting condition.'

Landon pursed his lips. 'I'd have to run that past our underwriting department, and corporate benefit office. Please understand that since you'd be listed as a contractor, that will be harder to pull off.'

'I understand, but I hope you can make it work. Even if it's only partial coverage, anything is better than nothing,' Howard offered.

'Anything else you need?' Landon asked.

'I'll need passage back to Earth after the mission is over.'

Landon let out a low whistle. 'You are driving one heck of a hard bargain here Captain. There won't be any regular liner's for months after the colony is set up.'

'I will ride back in a cargo barge if I have to, I just can't afford to be away for as long as I normally would.'

'You do understand that normally the Captain takes part in colonial administration after the mission is completed. This is a colony mission after all.'

'I do understand that, and I wish I could be more accommodating than this, but I have extenuating circumstances.'

Landon nodded again. 'Well Captain Fredrick, I know how much we were hoping to have you lead this mission. While I can't promise you any outcomes, I can promise that I'll try. I can try and get you an answer for the first and third conditions right away, but the second will take more doing.'

'I would appreciate it.'

'I'll call you back then,' Landon said.

'Thank you.'

'Talk to you later.'

'Goodbye,' Howard said, switching off the call.

He turned to his wife, 'I guess we wait now.'

'I guess so. What if they don't bite?'

'We'll see how much they come back with, something is better than nothing,' Howard offered.

'I was hoping you'd say that,' she said with a smile.

CHAPTER ONE

<u>NEW HORIZONS</u>

Lomard Shipyard

The sun was just cresting over the curve of the Earth. A wall of light started near the top of the wall and worked its way down as the space station continued its rotation around the planet below. Howard Fredrick, crisp in his Axion uniform, raised a hand to his eyes to block some of the light.

This was a familiar sight. He'd seen thousands of such sunrises in his career in space. Still, he did enjoy taking a quiet moment from time to time to appreciate their beauty. Even now, with humanity reaching across the stars, the number of people who got to see this, truly see this, was in the minority.

Howard looked down at his datapad, and called up the message that had brought him here up here.

'Dear Captain Fredrick

'I found out about your wife while trying to get her covered by our employee benefits. I want to offer you my condolences.

'If I had known that she was suffering as she was, I

wouldn't have been so impatient with your conditions. As it is, I'm glad that I can help you out with that situation in at least some small way.

'You know we already accepted two of your conditions, we were just waiting for news from our corporate benefits department for the last one.

'I'm pleased to say that heart beat out over cold business this time. Though our insurance provider is unwilling to cover your wife's condition, we at Axion are willing to offer you a dollar match for her next batch of treatments with Doctor Patel.

'I spoke with the Doctor at some length, and he told me about his research and how much hope he has in this new treatment for your wife's degenerative muscular disorder. He stressed how this could be a game changer.

'As such, we just couldn't pass up this chance to do something good, not only for you and your wife but for the future as well. Our contributions will help him continue his research.

'So in short, for every dollar, you spend on this, we'll match it, giving you an effective fifty percent discount. Beyond that, we'll be helping Doctor Patel with further funding after that, but that's between him and us.

'I hope this is acceptable to you, we eagerly await your reply.

'Landon Richards

'Head of Human Resources

'Axion Data Systems'

It had been acceptable. Howard and his wife had been happy with the result and had eagerly accepted. Howard looked up from the pad and smiled. He looked back out the window.

'Howard Fredrick?'

Howard turned to the sound of his name being called. A thin man with short black hair was walking toward him. He had a data pad under his arm and smile on his face.

Howard held out his hand to shake, and the man took it eagerly.

'I'm afraid you have me at a disadvantage, you are?' Howard asked.

'Keith Loheim, chief enginer for the *Azure Dream*.'

Howard nodded. 'On my crew then. Pleasure to meet you.'

'And you, Captain. I read your personnel file when I signed on for the mission. You have a very impressive dossier.'

Howard smiled. 'Years of not dying is what that amounts to. I didn't do anything spectacular really.'

'You got your jobs done and your crews home, even when things went wrong. You served on some of early Jump Drive equipped ships. That took a special kind of person.'

'It took someone with a strong sense of wanderlust,' Howard said.

Keith nodded, and looked out the window. He raised a hand and then looked down.

'Oh wow, that's the ship isn't it?'

Howard walked closer to the window and looked down too. Beneath them, the shadow shape of the hull of a ship stretched out in among the spiderlike arms of the ship yard complex they were in. With the sun shinning in their eyes, it was hard to make out details, but then the sun slipped under the shape of the craft, and it was lit with a glow from behind. The station lights pointed on the hull gave them a view of the equipment still being put in place. As they watched, a large container was being manoeuvred into place by small pod like ships.

'That must be it. The *Azure Dream*,' Howard said quietly. That was to be his home for the next four months.

'It's bigger in person. You hardly get a real sense of the scale until you see it.'

Howard glanced at his watch. Keith noticed him and grinned.

'We're late aren't we?' Keith asked.

'Not if we move quick. Board Room 3 is just down this passageway. Besides, I doubt they'll get to anything really juicy without me there.'

Keith nodded and together they set off, down the passage and to a waiting meeting

Lombard Ship Yard, Board Room 3

'Captain Fredrick, Mr. Loheim, glad you could make it,' said a beaming Landon Richards.

Two men walked into an already full board room. At one end of a long table, a man in a pinstriped suit stood with his back to a projector display. The display showed a upper case blue 'A' in a the centre of a circle of black. It was the Axion Data System Logo. Beneath it were the words 'Future Proof'.

The two men took seats around the table. Landon continued with his presentation.

'As all of you here are no doubt aware, Axion Data Systems has decided to fund a new colonization project for the International Space Agency. Axion takes this responsibility very seriously, and only the finest equipment has been secured for this ship. We have hand picked the crew from a pool of rigorously tested candidates. As per your mission contracts each of you will be the department heads for this mission.

'Most of you already know Captain Howard Fredrick. Captain Fredrick will be commanding this mission. He has years of experience behind him, having commanded many missions both in the private sector and for government organizations. This will be Captain Fredrick's first colony mission, but we at Axion are excited to have a man of his experience on our team.'

The presenter smiled a well practised smile and

continued his presentation. He clicked a pointer in his hand. The image being displayed by the projector changed. It showed a camera feed of the *Azure Dream,* sitting nestled in the arms of the space dock. Its new hull plating gleamed in the sunlight.

It had two distinct sections separated by long scaffold beams running from one section to the other. The beams connected from the bottom corners, and the top centre of the ship.

'This is the *Azure Dream.* She will be your home for the next few months. She is our pride and joy. The newest and most advanced ship of the Axion fleet. Packed stem to stern with the finest colonial infrastructure our not inconsiderable resources can buy.

'As many of you know, this same basic design has been used, with only minor adjustments, over the past ten years of human kinds colonization,' the presenter said. 'You can see here on the display, the core of the ship is mostly complete. The large space between the two sections will be filled up by the modular bays that will house all the colonists and colonial infrastructure. Presently we've started loading the bays.' He pointed to the one Howard had seen being manoeuvred earlier, 'This is one of the living quarters bays being positioned now.'

Landon moved to a new camera feed, this one focusing on the front of the ship. The front section of the ship was wide at the back, and tapered forward and downwards, forming a kind of curving nose section, like the front of an airplane.

'The forward section houses the command and control systems, including the bridge and the Guardian Control Room. This is also the area where the bulk of the crew quarters and storage areas are located,' the presenter said.

Along the hull of the front section, there were sensors and communication arrays being attached by the work crews.

'As you can see, there's still some last minute work to be done. A lot of the external equipment still needs to be attached.'

Landon switched the camera, now it displayed the back section of the ship.

'The aft section of the ship houses the engineering bay and the ship's engines. When I say engines, I do mean both the sub light engines and the jump drives.'

A hand went up.

'Yes, Mr Loheim?'

'How do we get from engineering to the bow section when there's no modules to walk through?'

'When the space between the aft and bow sections is empty like this, there's a pair of retractable corridors that can be used to connect the two sections of the ship. Granted, it'd be a bit of a walk, but it'll get the job done. Of course, in an emergency, you could always get in a space suit and walk along this bit here.' Landon pointed at a large metal strut that stretched from the bow to the aft section along the top of the ship. 'The designers call the this the spine. This is where the power, oxygen, and waste systems run through to feed the colony modules once they're all in.

'But all that aside, the cherry on top of this multi-billion dollar sundae is XO-33. The newest christened core of our XO line of Guardian cores. The XO series has been used extensively in ship based capacities, everything from deep space transports, to survey ships, with a few patrol cruisers thrown in for good measure. All without a hitch.'

Keith raised his hand again.

'Yes, Mr Loheim?'

'Has an XO core ever been used on a colony ship before?' asked Keith.

'First time for everything. The cores have undergone extensive virtual testing simulating journeys of much greater length and every kind of problem we could think of. As we expected, all the tests came up well within expected parameters.

'And in the event of a core shut down, there's still enough manual systems on board that the ship could be flown by the crew without assistance from the core.' Landon almost beamed with pride, and then continued, 'But the jump calculations would take forever. Ideally you'd just send a message on the long range array, and we'll come to pick you up.

'Incidentally, there is another colony ship called *Fallow*

Fields that's being equipped with an XO model. It will be departing a month after the *Azure Dream*.'

Keith nodded.

Landon took a sip of water from a glass on the table and then switched the picture on the screen. It showed a blue green world with unfamiliar land masses, orbiting a star much like the sun.

'This is Veil.'

'That's an interesting name choice,' Captain Fredrick said.

Landon nodded. 'It is, someone had been feeling poetic at the time of giving it a name. I understand it's because it's near a nebula that's particularly thick. Almost impossible to see through with our instruments.'

Another hand went up. This one from the first officer, Mark Jona.

'Mr. Jona, you have a question?'

'Yes, what sort of data do we have on this world?'

'Initial surveys by scouts on contract from Light-Lines Incorporated are very promising. A twenty seven hour rotational period. An orbital period of four hundred and eighty two local days. Temperature variance during the seasons is a a touch more extreme in the temperate and arctic regions, as the planet has a more axial tilt than Earth.

'Spectral analysis shows a breathable atmosphere. Gravity is about 1.1 times that of the earth. Atmospheric pressure is a bit higher. All in all, a golden find. It also has two small moons in orbit around it.'

Mark interrupted, 'Was there a ground based survey?'

'Yes, a survey was carried out by EverSky Surveys. However, it was very limited, which focused on potential colony sites. There were a few choice locations that were looked at.'

'Why was it a limited survey?' Mark asked.

'Unfortunately, due to the distance from Earth, or the next major colony, supplies were an issue. As well as since the orbital survey and environmental reports didn't show anything glaringly wrong, it was decided we could just do a focused survey of the areas in question.'

Howard raised his hand.

'Yes, Captain Fredrick?'

'What kind of infrastructure are we bringing with us?' Howard asked, while flipping to the appropriate section in his info package.

'Glad you asked, Captain. I was going to get to that next.

'As I mentioned earlier, the space between the aft and bow sections is going to be filled by modular colony bays. Each of the bays are self contained reentry vehicles. When the *Azure Dream* hits orbit, the bays will be sealed, and dropped to the planet. Once on the ground they'll act as the starting infrastructure for the colony. The bays will be converted into greenhouses, residential blocks, and other facilities.

'The other part of the colonial puzzle is the sustainable power grid. The largest bay on the ship serves a twofold purpose. It houses the solar power arrays that will be put in orbit around Veil, and the bay itself will serve as a core for the first space station for the colony.'

Landon moved to the next slide. An animated clip showed the lowest and largest bay detaching from the ship and moving into orbit. As the clip went on, it showed a solar power array being built in orbit.

'Once in orbit, the bay will be detached from the ship first, along with a small crew equipped for zero-g construction. They'll set up the solar power array in orbit, and then the colony will set up a receiver station. The power will then be transmitted from orbit to the ground station via a microwave tranmitter, and converted to usable power.'

'Excuse me,' Keith interrupted, 'but what happens if we can't set up the array?'

'In the event that the solar array cannot be set up, the ship can land, and the onboard generators can power the colony for up to year on their own. After that time, the generators will need to receive additional fuel, but of course, by then we should have sent additional supplies to the colony.' Keith raised his hand. 'But before you ask if something goes really wrong, Axion will dispatch an emergency courier to the colony if you don't check in within two weeks after your scheduled departure time.'

'Two weeks is quite some time to wait on an alien

world,' Captain Fredrick commented.

'It is indeed, but unfortunately, it could be even longer, as the nearest ships would still need time to get supplies and get there, as well as receive orders from Axion in the first place. Worst case, it could be up to two months before anyone checks in.'

Landon raised his hands to stave off any additional questions. 'I know what your thinking, that's a long time to be on your own, and I'm not going to deny that, but you literally have everything you need to survive, even without power, for those two months. In the event that you lose that ability, well I don't think a scout ship is going to do much to save you. A disaster of that magnitude would probably mean the ship had been rendered completely inoperable. Regrettably, there's not really any recovery from that. Space flight has always been a risky business after all.'

Captain Fredrick said, 'That's true enough. We'll just have to make sure it doesn't get to that point.'

'Thank you, Captain. That about concludes the introduction, unless we have any other questions, we can get into the specifics.'

Mark Jona was flipping through his information folder. 'I have a question. I know Guardian Cores require an Advocate. Who is our Advocate?'

Landon looked down at his notes. 'Ahh, I guess I didn't mention that yet.' He reached down to the display built into the table and hit a few keys. The big screen behind him displayed the personnel file for the Advocate.

'This is Samuel Jennings.' The picture of Samuel showed off the otherness of his skin, the odd colour of his eyes, and the perfect nature of his hair. 'As most of you know, due to the highly advanced nature of the A.I. Guardian cores, normal human interactions have proven to be too slow and cumbersome when attempting to teach them. As such, human kind created the Advocates cybernetically enhanced humans capable of keeping up with the Guardian's while they learn how to interact with humans.'

'He looks odd,' said Keith.

'The cybernetic enhancements that Samuel underwent gives him many other capabilities beyond interacting with the Guardian. His skin isn't actually skin, but is a flexible, yet very strong alloy. It'll allow him to survive in conditions far harsher than you or I could, which will be useful in the event of ship wide system failures, as it'll allow him to still access the core. His eyes are completely artificial and have much greater visual acuity than we do,' the presenter said.

'And his hair?' Keith asked.

'That's just cosmetic. His brain has had various hardwired implants added to it, with ports being embedded in his skull. The hair is more like a toupee, which is meant to cover the ports. Normally the Advocate can just talk to the Guardian over a wireless system, but if that system should ever fail, he'd need a hardwired option to interface.

Those particular data ports take care of that. But we've found that people find them distasteful so it's easier to hide them with the hair.

'Now, if there are no further questions, it's about time we separate. Each of you will be meeting with your departments and have more detailed briefings about your tasks on the ship. The *Azure Dawn* is set to depart in three months. Plenty of work to do before then gentlemen, I suggest we get cracking.'

The crew got up and started to file out of the room.

CHAPTER TWO

FIRST JUMP

Azure Dream – Earth Orbit

'Captain Fredrick, you have a green light for your exit vector.'

Three months had passed since the initial briefing at Axion Data Systems. Captain Howard found himself standing on the command deck of the *Azure Dream*. Howard looked over his command crew before they set off on their journey. Though the crew had been picked by Axion Data Systems, the sponsor of the mission, he had come to know all of them during the preparation.

He had infact gotten to know everyone, except for two. One wasn't so bad, but the other one set him on edge.

The two in question were the Guardian and the Advocate supplied by their corporate sponsors at Axion Data Systems.

The Advocate, Samuel Jennings, was standing on the bridge with his arms folded and a broad smile on his face. He was excited about this trip, and it clearly showed. It wasn't his first time into space, but it was his first time into deep space. It was always a special experience to go past the confines of the solar system. Howard noticed that he could see some of the signs of his implants under his mop of hair. His skin also had an odd sheen in the light of the bridge.

Earth was still new to the game of owning worlds. Thus far, it seemed as though they were alone. They had not met with any other intelligent life. Though life itself was surprisingly common, now that man walked the surface of distant worlds. Human space was full of new examples of Flora and Fauna, and Howard reflected on how blessed he was to be alive at such a time.

He'd seen a few of these new species himself, with his own eyes, having been across human space a number of times over his career.

And of course, that was only made possible by the advances mankind had made in the field of artificial intelligence. The advances like the Guardians and Advocates.

'Advocate Jennings, how are you holding up so far?' Captain Fredrick asked amicably.

'I am fantastic, sir,'

'Just Howard is fine.'

'Just Sam is fine for me then.'

'Alright, Sam,' Howard said with a smile. The Advocates were technically equal to a ship captain in rank, though standard procedure gave the final say to the captain in times of emergency.

'You've done this before, Captain. Yet you still seem to

be excited by it,' Sam commented.

'It's true. It's hard not to be excited by this. The things I've seen and done over my lifetime would be things of fantasy to my great grandparents. Even a hundred years go, when we first set out with our first jump drives and primitive AI, this would seem like an impossible dream. We're crossing four hundred light years in a matter of months. Not *years*.'

'When you say it like that, yeah, it does have some weight to it. I'm happy to do my part of course.'

'You'd better, Sam. I'm not really a big fan of Guardians you know. I wish I could say otherwise, but I suppose I'm just an old fashioned sort of man. If this wasn't my last mission, I'd worry about them putting me out of a job.'

Now it was Samuels turn to smile. 'Captain, I understand your feelings. I've run into it a lot actually. And let's not forget there are people who have gone far further in their dislike. The Anti-A.I. League wouldn't hesitate to destroy every Guardian in existence.'

'I'm not that far gone. Without them, jump calculations would be next to impossible.'

Sam nodded. 'Exactly. And just so you are aware, of the other 32 XO series Guardian cores, none of them developed any serious problems. In fact, they've all performed better than expected. Axion outdid themselves on this model.'

'Seeing as they're the ones that made the first real Guardian core, I'd hope their experience was paying off,'

Howard commented.

He thought for a moment before saying, 'Have you ever worked with an XO series before?'

Sam shook his head. 'No, this will be my first. The last series I worked with was the PE series.'

'I hope you are up to it.'

'I should be. I'll have access to the Axion technical database if I need it.'

'Never much cared for how things are now. I remember the older Guardian's. They were little more than glorified jump computers with attitude.'

'Never heard it put quite like that before,' Sam said with a smile.

Howard nodded. 'Some of the old ones weren't as good with human interaction as they are now. Personaly if I had had the choice, I would have signed on with a mission without a core. Unfortunatly, this is what I was offered, so here I am.'

'Lucky for us, we're fortunate to have a captain of your calibre here.'

Howard smiled. 'We'd better get ourselves underway, Sam.'

He turned to helmsman at the front of the bridge.

'What's the status of our drive systems?' Captain Fredrick asked his helmsman

'Fully operational, and ready for full burn,' came the reply.

'Very well, take us out of orbit. Comm, confirm flight plan with space control and then lock it in.'

The two crew members at the navigation and helm stations gave their acknowledgement.

'*Azure Dream* to space traffic control, we confirm green light, and we are ready to depart.'

'Roger that *Azure Dream*. Godspeed.'

'We'll check in when we pass the Oort cloud and begin our long range jumps.'

'Roger that,' replied the controller.

The view of the Earth filling their view screens, rotated away as the ship's pilot turned the ship onto its exit vector.

Sam was smiling again. 'It's exciting to be underway. I've never been as far as we're going.'

Howard smiled. 'Glad you're so excited Sam. You'll keep that Guardian under control for me right?'

Sam laughed. 'You don't need to worry. The Guardians haven't failed yet, and I don't plan on sullying that record on my watch.'

'Good to hear. Though I reckon we could fly this ship without its help.'

'I don't doubt your abilities, Captain. You have a very impressive record.' Sam looked back to the main screen, and the display of the flight path out of orbit, 'I hope to be able to lessen your misgivings about the Guardians.'

From the helm came a voice, 'Exit vector engaged, we'll be in safe jump distance momentarily.'

'Set the first jump for Io Supply station,' Howard ordered.

'Roger that, Captain,' the navigation officer said.

'Captain, all systems are green. Jump systems ready for an inter-system jump,' reported the helmsmen.

'Engage.'

With a flicker of something just beyond the range of vision and a split second feeling of overwhelming vertigo, the grand giant of Jupiter snapped into view. The curvature of Jupiter's moon, Io, took up the bottom third of the screen. A collection of lights sat floating right above it. The lights were from the Axion Data Systems Io Station. It was the first permanent installation built in the Jupiter orbital region, and it was a hub of activity for many of the corporations and private firms in the area. The swirling clouds of Jupiter sat as a glorious backdrop.

'*Io* station to *Azure Dream*, please make your approach on Vector One-Three.' said a voice over the speakers, 'Proceed to Holding Zone 8. Delivery of your Guardian and final supplies will commence once you are in position.'

'Roger that Io Station. *Azure Dream* inbound on Vector One-Three,' replied the comm officer.

Howard turned towards Sam. 'Well, from here on out, you and the Guardian take care of the jump calculations.

'You'll still have plenty to do Howard, but you know as well as I do that if there are any mistakes in the long range jumps we could miss our target planet. Trying to find it again without the assistance of a survey ship would be unpleasant.'

'But not impossible,' Howard countered. 'Our navigator, Irwin Fritz, used to be a stellar cartographer and is quite familiar with the star charts of the area.'

'Ahh, we are in good hands then,' Sam said.

The ship started moving toward the space station floating in orbit above Io. It slowly started to resolve itself into a ring-shaped structure with spokes coming out of the ring at regular intervals. At the end of most of the spokes there sat the huge forms of various tankers and barges moving resources and supplies around the Jovian industrial complexes.

'Come on, Sam, let's go see the Guardian. The station technicians will be bringing it online.'

...

...

SYSTEM START.

XO-33 GUARDIAN.

V3.7.11

SEARCHING FOR ADVOCATE UPLINK.

...

...

ADVOCATE UPLINK FOUND.

ADVOCATE DESIGNATION; SAMUEL JENNINGS.

ACCESS CLEARANCE; FULL ACCESS, COMMAND AUTHORIZATION.

ACTIVATING FULL ADVOCATE UPLINK.

SENDING AUTHORIZATION CODES.

...

ADVOCATE CODES RECEIVED.

'HELLO XO-33. BRING *AZURE DREAM* UPLINK ONLINE. RUN FAMILIARIZATION PROGRAMMING, AND COME MEET THE CAPTAIN,' SAM SAID OVER THE WIRELESS LINK BETWEEN HIM AND THE GUARDIAN.

ACTIVATING SHIP UPLINK.

ACCESSING LANGUAGE FILES.

ACTIVATING INTERACTION PROGRAMMING.

...

'He's waking up now Captain,' Sam said.

In a large room with a clear pillar in the centre of it, Howard and Sam stood to wait.

The pillar seemed to waver for a moment before it was filled by the holographic image of a human head. The head looked narrow in build and had very sharp check bones.

'Hello, Captain Howard Fredrick. I am XO-33, Guardian core assigned to the *Azure Dream*,' said the head.

'Are you going to listen to Sam here all the way to our destination XO-33?' Howard asked quickly.

'I am programmed to listen to the commands of Advocate at all times.'

'See that you do. If push comes to shove I am more than willing to fly this ship myself.'

'That would not be recommended, Captain. The complexity of the jump calculations over the distances we are travelling would make such a feat considerably mo-' the head was silent for a moment, 'I... I mean I will listen to Samuel at all times sir.'

Howard frowned and looked at Sam, who just smiled a wry grin.

'Did you just tell him to...?' Howard let the rest of the sentence to go unfinished.

'I'd rather not comment,' Sam said with the same grin.

Howard turned back to XO-33.

'Am I going to have to call you XO-33 all the time?'

'I am programmed to accept "Nicknames" so long as they are determined ahead of time.'

Howard looked at his feet for a moment. 'How about Exo?' he asked looking up.

'Nickname has been logged.'

'Okay then. Exo it is,' Howard said.

'It is what?' asked the head.

'Never mind. So Exo, with your calculations, how big will every jump be?' Howard asked.

'Axion's estimate is at 40 light years. Distance will vary based on variables that may arise.'

'With jumps that long, how long is the drive going to take to recharge and reset?'

'Approximately 12 days between jumps.'

'Bit of a delay between jumps,' Howard commented.

Sam piped in, 'That's because of the distances involved. With Exo doing the calculations we are increasing the range of the jumps by almost twice what we could safely do with a human only crew. We'll end up cutting the total travel time by about two months.'

Howard turned to Sam. 'We've still got four months of travel to cover. But we've got all the colonial supplies. We could take longer if needed.'

'Hopefully, nothing goes wrong,' Sam said.

'I may not like all the factors of this expedition, but it's been done before. We are far from the first to try colonising. We're just the first to go this far. So long as we're all doing our jobs we should be fine,' Howard said.

'Yes Captain, but the last ship to colonise was the first to go out as far as it did, and the one before that was the first to go out as far as it did. We'll be fine.

Exo's head dropped its chin, then looked back up at Sam and the Captain. 'Io Station reports supply loading is complete. The last of the specialists have finished disembarking. We are ready to get under way.'

'Alright. Sam, let's get to the bridge.'

Past The Oort Cloud

'Jump drive offline. Commencing recharge sequence,' the voice of XO-33 said flatly from the bridge speakers. 'ETA till next jump, 30 minutes. The jump will be four point five light years in distance.'

'That's a short jump,' Sam commented.

Howard looked over at him. 'We're still close enough to Sol that we are receiving interference from the sun. Stronger gravity wells do strange things to the Jump drive's accuracy, so we don't want to jump too far on the first jump. We'll be able to get our bearings with that short of a jump, correct for our drift, and then make a maximum distance jump far away from the effects of Sol. Once we're in the space between the stars, there is very little interference to throw us off.

'We have a slightly shorter recharge time for the first few jumps. Once the stresses start to build up in the drive arrays, we'll have to wait longer between jumps. It's a very tricky procedure. After every jump, the drive receives a residual charge that can interfere with further jumps. So before we recharge the drive, we've got to bleed off that charge. Hence, why we have a shorter recharge on the first jump, there hasn't been enough time to build a charge yet.'

'Interesting. I did not know that. I've never been outside the solar system before,' Sam said, 'so nothing like that has come up.'

'Nothing quite like it. I've been across human space a number of times. Once I went to a fascinating place, a facility called Twilight.'

'Oh, what was that like?'

'It's mostly a research station. The star it orbits is strange. It's cooled and crystallised. The Twilight station is there to study it. At the time I was there they were trying to... well I don't know the science of it, but basically tune into the thing. Like using a crystal transmitter on an old radio. They were going to see if they could use it like a massive receiver.'

'How will they be able to be able to pick out anything meaningful from all the background noise?'

'As I understood it, every now and again, they have a neighbouring colony make radio broadcasts in their direction, and then they see if they can pull it out of all the background noise. Since they already know what the signal is going to look like, it helps them get their tuning just right. Once they've got it figured out, they should be able to start figuring what's interesting, and what's just noise.'

'That sounds fascinating,' Sam said.

'I'll leave it to the scientists. That sort of thing always interested me, but I was never any good at it,' Howard said. 'Well, you've got some time to kill. Why don't you go have a look around the ship?'

'I don't mind if I do,' Sam said and started walking.

CHAPTER THREE
NEVER ALONE

Outside Bridge

Walking down the long passages of the ship, Sam was never truly alone. His constant companion, the Guardian, was always watching him, and ever present in his mind.

'EXO?' SAM ASKED OVER THE LINK.

'YES, ADVOCATE?'

'DIRECT ME TO AN OBSERVATION AREA,' SAM REQUESTED.

'PROTOCOL INDICATES THAT YOU SHOULD NOT EXPOSE YOURSELF TO UNNECESSARY RISK. OBSERVATION AREAS ARE THE LEAST SHIELDED ON THE SHIP.'

'WE ARE NOT MOVING. THE LAST ACCIDENT IN RELATION TO AN OBSERVATION AREA WAS OVER FORTY YEARS AGO AND THAT WAS WHILE MOVING. I'LL BE FINE,' SAM SAID.

'YES, ADVOCATE. FOLLOW MY DIRECTIONS.'

Sam walked on in silence. To the outside observer, he appeared to know exactly where he was going. Inside his quiet exterior, though, Sam was being given directions as he walked.

Soon he found himself in a large round room that was ringed with windows. The Windows weren't made of glass, but a clear material of much greater strength.

Sam walked up to one of the curved windows. He was on top of the ship, near the back, overlooking the length of the craft.

He gazed out at the ship and the stars.

'EXO, WHICH STAR IS SOL?' SAM ASKED.

'IT WILL BE THE STAR THAT IS THREE FEET ABOVE THE SECOND DRIVE NOZZLE. I WILL INDICATE IT.

Samuel looked down the length of the ship to the two visible drive nozzles of the conventional engines used to move the ship around when it completed a jump or was approaching a planet.

Above the drive nozzle was a small point of light with a faint red circle displayed around it by Exo through Sam's eyes. It was nothing at all like a grand ball of light worshipped as a God by ancient people. It's distance and diminished size stirred something in Sam, an odd sense of loss. It was akin to saying goodbye to an old friend.

'ADVOCATE. WE WILL BE COMMENCING OUR NEXT JUMP IN TWO MINUTES. I SUGGEST YOU TAKE A SEAT. THIS WILL BE A LONGER JUMP, AND WE DO NOT KNOW THE EFFECTS OF THE JUMP

SICKNESS ON YOU YET,' EXO SAID.

'THANK YOU, EXO.'

Sam walked over to one of the couches in the room. Each one looked perfectly normal, but also doubled as a crash restraint, with safety harnesses built into them out of the way but accessible in the event of an emergency.

Sam took a seat, and strapped in for good measure, looking out at the back of the ship. He kept an eye on Sol.

The seconds ticked on, then everything seemed to become tinted with a shade of purple. All the stars dimmed and vanished. Then, in a fraction of a second, new ones snapped into place where they had been. The colour faded and Sam was left staring at an empty spot in space where Sol had been, fighting an intense desire to throw up.

The sickness was over almost as soon as it began, and Sam stood up.

'TIME UNTIL THE NEXT JUMP?' SAM ASKED

'APPROXIMATELY TWENTY-FOUR HOURS.'

'RUN A FULL SYSTEM DIAGNOSTIC ON ALL HIGH-LEVEL COMMAND LINKS. THAT SHOULDN'T INTERFERE WITH YOUR JUMP CALCULATIONS SHOULD IT?' SAM ASKED

'I WILL BE PERFORMING MOST OF THE CALCULATIONS INTERNALLY AND NOT RELYING ON SHIP SYSTEMS. THE HIGH-LEVEL COMMAND LINKS WILL BE UNUSED,' EXO ANSWERED

'PROCEED WITH THE TEST. I'LL BE GOING FOR A WALK FOR NOW.'

'YES, ADVOCATE,' EXO REPLIED.

Sam got up from the couch and left the lounge. Without guidance, he walked aimlessly among the decks. His enhanced body wouldn't require sleep for some time yet. He could always force his body into an idle state, but he had yet to familiarise himself with the ship as a whole or to meet any of the people on board.

Four months cooped up on a colony ship was not anyone's idea of a good time, but it was a far cry better than the old days of deep hibernation and years of transit. Care was taken to pick good candidates and to give them everything they needed to thrive and stay happy on the journey.

Sam stopped outside a double door in a hallway he had wandered down. The information panel said it was a theatre.

Sam hit the open button and walked in.

A fairly spartan lobby was on the other side of the door. A ticket desk was manned by a bored looking blond haired lady. She had blue eyes and a round face. She was flipping through a book and leaning back in her seat.

Sam realised he was probably older than her by a good twenty years. The nature of the enhancements given to him increased his life span.

She heard him come in and looked up. She looked a little surprised at his presence.

'You're the Advocate aren't you?' she said.

'Yes, but please call me Sam. And your name is?'

'I'm Sarah. How can I help you, sir?'

Sam held up his hands and said, 'Please, just Sam. No sirs for me.'

She smirked at this and seemed to relax. 'Okay then Sam. What can I do for you?'

'What is this place?'

'It's a movie theatre. Though we'll also use it for plays or musical programs if anyone on board feels like producing any. I imagine there will be more of those once we reach Veil.'

'I see. Is anything good on?'

'The next program isn't for another hour. Most people don't like being interrupted mid-program by a jump. Nausea tends to spoil the show,' Sarah matter-of-factly.

'I can understand why,' Sam replied cheerily.

'Would you care to get an advanced ticket?'

'How does your ticket system work? How do you ensure everyone gets a show?' Sam asked, leaning on the counter.

'It's a first come first serve system, with a quota attached. If there is an overbooking, the people who have seen the least number of programs here will get priority seating, to ensure that it's fair.'

'And this is your job?'

She chuckled, 'Oh this would get very boring for four months. I also work in the hydroponic bays. I'm one of the technicians. I make sure all the plants are healthy, happy, and nutritious.'

'A farmer of sorts then,' Sam said with a grin.

'My father was a farmer on Earth, I hated the dirt,' she said with a sour face. 'Now I farm in space with nothing but powered lighs. water, and scientific instruments. What about you, Sam? Were you always an Advocate? I always wanted to meet an Advocate.'

Sam smiled. 'Most Advocates are picked while still young. It's a lifelong journey to learn with and teach the Guardians. They are in a way like children when they first come online. Our own Guardian XO-33 is a greenhorn. He's by no means incapable of doing his job, but he has yet to develop a personality.'

'A machine with a personality?' Sarah asked.

'Every Guardian develops one. I worked with one on the Lunar refineries that had this bizarre habit of speaking in a french accent. It drove the Axion programmers absolutely up the wall. Those guys couldn't figure out why, and the Guardian... what was its name... PE-6. Of course, we just called him Pierre.

'Pierre?' Sarah said with a smile. 'That's funny. What do you call our Guardian?'

'Well, its name is XO-33, but the Captain and I have decided to call him Exo.'

'Exo, eh? Can he hear us right now?'

'Well, he's always keeping tabs on me, but he's busy with a task I gave him.'

A monotone voice chimed in, 'I am here Advocate.'

Sarah looked at Sam with a sheepish grin.

Sam smiled back. 'Nothing to worry about Exo, we were just speaking about you.'

'Yes, Advocate,' said the voice.

'So *that* was Exo,' Sam said.

'Seems kind of stiff,' Sarah commented.

'Oh just give him time, he'll unwind.'

'If he unwinds too much, he won't be able to keep time.'

Sam stared at her, his mouth open in a surprised smile. He started to chuckle. Sarah laughed.

'Wow. That was... that was *good*. There are two things I love, bad jokes, and old movies.' Sam put on a mock serious face. 'Wouldn't happen to be playing any old classics tonight would you?'

'I'm afraid not.'

'Oh well, I feel like a movie anyway, so how about those tickets?' Sam said with a grin.

...

ADVOCATE UPLINK MUTED.

COMMENCE DATABASE SEARCH.

Arlin Fehr

CREW MEMBER DATABASE ACCESSING...

SEARCHING FILES...

SEARCH PARAMETERS.

NAME; SARAH

JOB; HYDROPONICS TECHNICIAN/ THEATRE ATTENDANT

SEARCHING...

SUBJECT FOUND.

NAME; SARAH LOUGH

AGE; 34

GENDER; FEMALE

MARITAL STATUS; SINGLE

ETHNICITY; U.S.A, IDAHO. CAUCASIAN.

ACCESS CERTIFICATIONS...

EDUCATION COMPLETED IN CHOSEN FIELDS.

ANALYSING RESULTS...

TEST SCORES ABOVE AVERAGE BUT NOT PERFECT

INTELLIGENCE AND PROBLEM-SOLVING SKILLS ABOVE

AVERAGE.

PHYSICAL PROWESS ADEQUATE.

ACCESSING MEDICAL FILE...

PASSED AXION MEDICAL EXAMS

PASSED I.S.A MEDICAL EXAMS

NO GENETIC OR CONGENITAL DEFECTS REPORTED.

SUITABILITY AS MATE FOR ADVOCATE: ACCEPTABLE

SAVING RESULTS...

...

UNMUTING ADVOCATE UPLINK

'HELLO, EXO. WHERE DID YOU GO OFF TO?' SAM ASKED OVER HIS LINK

'JUST RUNNING AN ANALYSIS ON DATA. NEEDED TO DEVOTE MY FULL ATTENTION TO IT.'

'KEEP UP THE GOOD WORK, EXO. I'LL BE IN A MOVIE.'

'HAVE A GOOD TIME, ADVOCATE.'

'LET ME KNOW HOW THE ANALYSIS GOES,' SAM REPLIED.

Arlin Fehr

'Yes, Advocate.'

CHAPTER FOUR

<u>DAILY LIFE</u>

Bridge

Captain Howard was reading over the supply manifest as the bridge crew did a quick test of all the vital systems. He had thought it better they do that now when they were still relatively close to Earth and still deep in human space, rather than when they were half way to the destination like protocol demanded.

Not that the ship hadn't been thoroughly examined before it left earth orbit, but having the lives of numerous colonists on his hands was making him cautious.

Finishing up the cargo manifest, Howard waved over a bridge officer and handed her the manifest.

'Everything looks good, Lieutenant Yin. See that the department heads report in before the end of the day.'

'Yes Captain,' she said before turning around and leaving.

Standing up, Howard started to walk around the bridge. He stopped next to his first officer, Mark Jona.

'Mark, what's the status of our tests?'

'Mostly coming out green.'

'Mostly?' Howard asked with a note of concern.

'Yes, sir. There's some latency in the command system for the conventional drives,' Mark answered, looking up from his station.

'A delay?'

'It's fairly minor. It shouldn't give us any problems. We've seen this sort of thing before in ships that had just brought their Guardians online. I asked XO-33 if he had any idea what it was about. He told me that Samuel told him to run a diagnostic on all his higher level command uplinks. It's probably due to that.'

'Sam must have had the same idea we did. Better to work out all the kinks in the system while we're still close to our home.'

'Yes, Captain.'

'Keep an eye on that Mr Jona, let me know if we run into any more oddities. We shouldn't need those engines until we reach Veil.'

'Aye, Captain.'

'To think, crossing 400 light years in four months. Our ancestors would be amazed,' Howard commented.

'As our Guardians get more sophisticated, they help us design better jump drives and perform more in-depth jump calculations,' Mark commented, 'And it shows no sign of slowing down. We'll keep going further and faster.'

'I just hope we can keep on top of this kind of

technology. Everything we make seems to have a habit of being both good and bad at the same time.'

'Maybe sir, but we've made it this far. We've got thousands of years of human history and survival instinct behind us.'

'Until we make something we can't manage anymore.' Howard glanced at one of Exo's display monitors.

Mark followed his gaze. 'We crossed that threshold a long time ago, sir. Long ago we stopped being able to do everything and became specialised. I know more about interstellar jump drives than most of humankind, but I couldn't write a song to save my life. I couldn't start a fire with two sticks and some dry grass. But with our faster than light travel and communication systems, we have easy access to the people who have skills we don't.'

Howard looked around the bridge once more. 'As you were Mr Jona,' he said as he turned to walk off.

He walked towards the display panel linked to XO-33.

'Exo?'

The panel flashed to life and Exo's narrow face appeared on screen. 'Yes, Captain Howard?'

'Where is Sam?'

'He is watching a movie, sir.'

'Ah, okay then, thank you.'

'Yes, Captain.' Exo's face vanished and the screen shut off.

Not wanting to interrupt Sam, Howard decided to go

check on the rest of the ship. As he left the bridge, he thought it might be good to check on the children's schooling. He thought that it would be in session by this point. With twenty hours left until the next jump, the classes should just be doing an orientation session rather than a real class. They would probably wait until the next 12-day jump recharge cycle to start classes in earnest.

Knowing his ship inside and out, Howard knew where the closest school room was. He took the lift off the bridge and down to the deck where the room was.

He walked up to the door to the room and hit the open button. It slid open. Young children ages five to seven were scampering about the well-lit room. Toys were in a few piles around the room. The teacher, a young lady with brown hair looked up from talking to two of the children.

'Oh, Captain Fredrick, what an unexpected surprise.'

'Hello.' Howard held out his hand and she shook it.

'My name is Mrs Lann, this is my classroom. To what do I owe the pleasure, Captain?'

'I'm just doing some rounds, I thought I'd stop by and introduce myself to some of the classrooms.'

'What a wonderful idea. Give me a minute to round everyone up.'

Many of the children had stopped and looked at Howard. Mrs Lann turned and motioned them around.

'Alright class, this is Captain Fredrick, he's the captain of our ship. He's the one in-charge of taking us to our new home.'

One of the kids looked up. 'Do you fly the ship all by yourself?'

Howard smiled. 'No no, I have many wonderful people working for me to help keep the ship going. It's far too big for just one person to take care of on his own.'

Mrs Lann looked at Howard. 'Will you be staying long, Captain Fredrick?'

'I can stay for a bit.'

'Alright, class, who would like to ask some questions to the Captain?'

A few hands went up. Howard picked a little blond girl with hazel eyes sitting in the front, 'You there.'

She lowered her hand and smiled, 'My daddy is an Advocate. Do we have one on our ship?'

Howard smiled at her. 'And what's your name little miss?'

'Ayla.'

'Well, Ayla, we do have one on this ship, his name is Samuel. He's a good man, and it's his job to keep our Guardian working. Where's your daddy, Ayla?'

Her face fell a little. 'Mommy say's he's gone far away. He used to work in the asteroids, but he got hurt bad and couldn't come home.'

Howard's own face fell a little as he recalled an incident about a year ago where a mining complex had been attacked by the Anti-A.I. League in a strike against the system. The

Advocate on the complex had died, sacrificing himself by using the Guardian and all the mining equipment to hold off the attackers while the complex workers evacuated. Howard suspected that that had been her father.

It didn't sound like Ayla knew that her dad died a hero, but Howard wasn't comfortable with taking over the job of parenting. Her mother had that job.

'I'm sorry to hear that, Ayla. Would you like to meet our Advocate one day?'

She nodded eagerly.

'I'll get him to come to class one day. Then you can meet him.' Howard looked at the rest of the children. 'Who else has questions?'

**

Finishing up with the questions, Howard stood to one side as the class ended and parents started to show up and gather their children. As the classroom cleared out, Howard walked over to the teacher. 'Excuse me, Mrs Lann, can I talk to you for a moment.'

'Of course Captain, and let me say, the children enjoyed having you.'

'I'll be sure to call ahead when I bring Sam to see them.'

'That will be delightful. Now, what would you like to know Captain?'

'That Ayla girl, what's her last name?'

'Geer. Ayla Geer.'

'That's what I thought. So it was her father involved in the attack last year,' Howard said thoughtfully.

'Yes. Her father was the one who saved all the workers. Tim Geer.'

'I don't suppose you know why her mother decided to come on this voyage do you?'

'When I saw the child's file, I had a meeting with her... I'm not sure I'm comfortable talking about it though, Captain. Everything she told me is in strict confidence.'

Howard brought a hand up to his face and placed it over his mouth, as he pondered this. 'Understandable. Alright, Mrs Lann, I've taken enough of your time. I'll let you get back home now.'

'Thank you, Captain. Any other time you want to stop by, please don't hesitate, the children love it.'

'I'll be back soon with Sam.'

'The students look forward to it, Captain.'

'Goodbye, Mrs Lann'

'Good bye, Captain Fredrick.'

Howard nodded, turned, and left. He looked at his watch, checking the time. An hour and a half had passed since he left the bridge. There were more classrooms in the ship, but there was no way he'd hit them all in one day. He'd have to get them later. The older students would be a different game altogether. They'd have harder questions.

'Exo?'

'Yes, Captain?'

'Is Sam done with his movie?'

'Yes, Captain.'

'Where is he now?'

'In one of the mess halls, with a friend.'

Howard raised his eyebrows. 'Is this friend a woman by any chance?'

'Yes, Captain.'

'Carry on Exo.'

'Yes, Captain.'

With a smile on his face, Howard walked down the hall, deciding not to go to the bridge. The second watch would be coming on duty in a few minutes. The third watch would be on duty for the next jump. Howard didn't think much would go wrong. He didn't feel the need to be on duty every time a jump happened. The crew was more than capable of calling him if the need arose. With Sam and Exo doing the lions share of the work, he didn't think much would go wrong. However much he may dislike the state of affairs with mankind and Guardians, Howard knew when not to fight.

As much as he didn't like to admit it, this mission would be much more difficult without Sam and Exo. The time cut off the journey meant they had more room on the ship for colonial infrastructure than if they had to pack for a longer journey.

Howard decided to take a walk down to one of the hydroponics bays. While the colonists learned how to farm on this new world, the massive bays would be the lifeblood of the colony.

His wife had a garden back on Earth. Their home near Winnipeg was out in the country.

Howard stopped in the hall for a moment as he thought of his wife, Sophie. She was still suffering from her condition, Doctor Pavel wasn't ready to start the treatment yet. Coming on this mission mean they could afford the treatment, but he'd been gone from home so long over his working life already.

He thought about that with a twinge of bitterness. If it hadn't been for his long voyages away, he may have had more time to spend with her. If the treatment didn't work, he might not see her again.

As it was, no one blamed him for coming on this journey. Those who knew why he was here encouraged him and told him to stay hopeful. He knew this was their only chance.

But still, he missed her.

Putting one foot forward to break his melancholy mood, he started to walk again. Already a man of sixty-six, he didn't have time to be wallowing in regret. Either this would work, or it wouldn't.

He wondered, for a moment, what he would do if the treatment didn't work. Life expectancy was closer to one hundered and ten years, so he would still have to make something of his life if Sophie wasn't going to be part of it anymore.

Maybe I'll come back to Veil. I could still make something of it with my time left, he thought.

Thinking of how much time he had left, he remembered that Sam would live much longer than him. Howard had a hard time thinking that Sam would be expected to live past two hundred. That must have an effect on Advocates and how they formed relationships, Howard thought. He made a decision to ask him about that sometime.

"Lo Captain.'

Howard looked up from his thoughts. It was one of the civilian directors in charge of some of the colonial infrastructure. Howard remembered his name was James Bennett.

'Hello, Mr Bennett. How goes the day?'

'Just heading off to take a look at the solar arrays. I noticed everyone seemed to be giving everything a once over, I thought I'd join in the fun.'

'Good man. Mind if I tag along?'

'Ahh, but 'tis your ship good sir. Feel free to tag along at your leisure. I may get you to do some work if you do,' James said with smile

'Any captain afraid to get his hands dirty ought not to be commanding a space ship I say,' Howard replied as they started to walk down the corridor.

'Some would say a captain is better used directing the labours of a ship,' James said, testing.

'We have our dear Guardians to do that these days,' Howard replied in a slightly mocking tone.

James smirked. 'Not a fan of the ol' metal men are you, sir?'

'They do their job, but there's not much of a job for an old astronaut these days.'

'Final grand adventure then is it, sir?'

'Something like that. I thought to myself that I need to get away from it all, it doesn't get much further than this.'

'Aye, it doesn't get much further at all. But you have to ask yourself, what if we just bring it all with us?'

Howard smiled a lopsided grin and looked to the side at the man. 'You are one of a kind Mr Bennett. Where are you from?'

'I hail from just outside of the fair city of Edinburgh, an' you can call me James sir, Mr Bennett was my father.'

'You can call me Howard, no need to stand on protocol, you're not part of my crew.'

'Nay, but I am on your ship.'

'So are a great many people who probably wouldn't recognise me if I was out of uniform.'

'Well, Howard, we're here. My little domain.' James said, standing outside of a large double door. He reached over and keyed the pad next to the door. The door slid open automatically.

'Little domain?' Howard said.

'Maybe a poor choice of words, I'll grant you,' James

said happily. 'As you can see, this bay is simply massive by comparison to the rest of the bays on this ship.'

James gestured around the bay, indicating the ten large solar arrays stacked tightly in the area.

'How large are those array's James?'

'Each one is about a kilometre long, and we've got them crammed in here like a cracker tin. A good idea these, we pop them out once we get to the planet, hook them together, and then beam down enough power for a buddin' colony. No fuel, no mess, and next to no maintenance. Perfect for those off the beaten path,' James said, smiling.

'Except maybe the size,' Howard mentioned.

James nodded, letting out a small laugh. 'Except maybe the size. We could have had a whole lot of supplies in here if it wasn't for them.'

Howard appreciated the idea behind the arrays nonetheless.

'So James, what are we going to do?'

'Well, I'm going to have a lot of time to work on these things between here and there, should the need come up, so I'm going to see which, if any, need work right now.'

'And how are we going to do that?'

'We'll be going on the maintenance scaffolding, and turnin' on the lights. Then we'll check and see if the panels pick up a charge. I only do it one array at a time, though. It takes a little while to get all the readings. No sense bitin' off more than one can chew.'

Wayward Guardian

'What should I do?'

'Well Captain, I'll show you.'

With that, Howard and James got to work.

CHAPTER FIVE

PASSAGE

Outside Sarah's Quarters

'Thank you, Samuel, this has been a lovely evening,' Sarah said with a smile. 'I'm glad you talked me into letting you treat me to a movie.'

Samuel returned the smile standing outside of the door to her quarters, having walked her back after dinner. 'The pleasure was all mine, Sarah. I'll see you again sometime, you have a good night.'

'You too Advocate,' she said, still smiling as she walked through the door.

As it shut behind her, Sam started to walk way, a smile on his lips.

'ADVOCATE?'

'YES, EXO?' SAM ANSWERED, OVER THE UPLINK.

'YOU DID NOT CEMENT THE RELATIONSHIP.'

Sam chuckled out loud

'PARDON?' SAM ASKED.

'MY STUDY OF HUMAN CULTURE SHOWS A NUMBER OF RITUALS TAKEN IN CEMENTING A RELATIONSHIP WITH A POTENTIAL MATE. MOST OF THE FILES WERE QUITE CONFUSING, BUT MY ANALYSIS SHOWS THAT YOU DID REMARKABLY LITTLE,' EXO OBSERVED.

'A MATE? EXO, YOU HAVE A BIT TO LEARN MY FRIEND.'

'WAS SHE NOT AN ACCEPTABLE MATE? MY ANALYSIS SHOWED HER TO BE ACCEPTABLE BY MOST HUMAN STANDARDS.'

'I'M NOT ONE TO TRIFLE WITH A RELATIONSHIP. ONE DOESN'T SIMPLY DO THINGS LIKE THIS FOR THE SAKE OF RITUAL, ' SAM REPLIED.

'HUMAN MATING RITUALS ARE NOT IN FULL AGREEMENT WITH YOU. THERE IS MUCH LITERATURE ON THE SUBJECT IN THE ARCHIVES. AND I HAVE OBSERVED AT LEAST SIXTEEN POSSIBLE ENCOUNTERS AMONG THE SHIP'S INHABITANTS WHILE YOU WERE BUSY. MANY VIDEOS AND CULTURAL RECORDS SHOW PEOPLE OFTEN TRIFLING WITH RELATIONSHIPS.'

'WHAT DO YOUR FILES SAY ABOUT MARRIAGE? '

'THERE IS MUCH DISAGREEMENT ABOUT THAT TOO. MANY CLAIM IT OLD FASHIONED AND UNESSENTIAL, A THROWBACK TO EARLIER TIMES. SOME CONSIDER IT RESTRICTING. '

'YET THERE ARE THOSE WHO STILL BELIEVE IT TO BE A GOOD THING ARE THERE NOT?'

'YES, ADVOCATE.'

'FOR NOW, LET'S JUST SAY THAT I AM ONE OF THOSE ONES WHO BELIEVES IT'S STILL A GOOD THING. WE'LL TALK ABOUT IT LATER, MAYBE ONCE WE REACH THE COLONY. '

'YES, ADVOCATE. WHAT SHOULD I ATTEMPT TO LEARN NEXT? '

'HOW ABOUT OBSERVING HUMAN INTERACTION ON THE SHIP. ANALYSE THE INTERACTIONS. COMPARE THEM TO YOUR FILES. MAKE ESTIMATES FOR OUTCOMES, AND THEN SEE HOW THEY UNFOLD. '

'YES, ADVOCATE.'

'IT'S NECESSARY YOU LEARN HOW TO UNDERSTAND PEOPLE AND WHY THEY DO THINGS. IT'LL HELP YOU SERVE THEIR NEEDS BETTER BECAUSE YOU'LL BE ABLE TO ANTICIPATE THEM,' SAM SAID.

'YES, ADVOCATE.'

'I'M GOING TO GO TO MY ROOM AND DO SOME READING. WHEN I'M DONE THAT I'LL PROBABLY GO TO BED. I DON'T REALLY NEED THE SLEEP, BUT I'D MUCH RATHER SLEEP THROUGH THE NEXT JUMP THAN TO BE AWAKE FOR IT. '

'I WILL WAKE YOU IF THERE IS AN EMERGENCY. '

'Good. good night, Exo.'

'Good night, Advocate.'

Bridge

The second jump had gone off without a hitch. The ship was now eight days into the twelve-day recharge. Captain Howard had been continuing his tour of the ship. He'd stopped at most of the school rooms on the ship, and had introduced himself to most of the civilian directors.

He remembered his promise to Mrs Lann's class. He'd have to find Sam and bring him down. He had told Sam about this, and the Advocate was looking forward to the experience.

Looking at his watch, he didn't think the class would be started yet if anything the children wouldn't be arriving for another hour, but Mrs Lann would certainly be there getting ready for her lessons.

Howard walked to a communication station and keyed her ID code. After waiting for a moment, the screen turned on and Mrs Lann was on the other side.

'Captain Fredrick,' she said with a smile, 'how can I help you?'

'I've been thinking about the promise I made to your class about bringing our Advocate down to meet them. Would today be a good day for that?'

'I didn't have anything particularly special planned

today, I think today would be just fine. When can we expect you?' she asked.

'When would you like us?'

'Oh well... Let's give the children a chance to settle in. How about a half hour after classes start?'

'Classes start in an hour right?' Howard said, glancing at his watch again.

'Yes.'

'Alright then Mrs Lann, we will see you then.'

'The children will be pleased.'

'Goodbye then.'

'Goodbye'

The communication screen shut off. Howard keyed in Sam's code this time.

Sam answered almost instantly. He was standing in one of the hydroponics bays. Howard could see the plants behind him.

'Hello, Howard. How are you today?' Sam said with a smile.

'I'm doing quite well. The ship and crew are working well, so there's not much for me to do. That said, you remember that visit to a school room I mentioned to you?'

'Ah yes, the class that wants to meet me.'

'That would be the one. Would you be willing to join me for that in about an hour and a half.'

Sam looked offscreen at an unseen person, and with an apologetic smile, shrugged his shoulders. Something was said offscreen and he smiled broadly. 'That should be just fine, Captain.'

'Oh, I don't mean to interrupt anything. You needn't change your plans.'

'Don't worry about it, Howard. The children are looking forward to meeting me, and I'm looking forward to meeting them.'

'Alright then, I'll see you there.'

The communication screen shut off and went black. Howard put his hands behind his back and faced the rest of the bridge again. The second watch would be coming on duty in an hour, then he'd have a half hour to make it down to the classroom.

'Mr. Jona.'

'Yes, Captain?' replied his first officer.

'Is that delay still present in the main drive systems?'

'Yes, Captain.'

'And we've talked to Exo about it?'

'I had Sam run a full diagnostic with Exo on the drive command systems. We've checked everything three times. I've got a crew looking over the connection physically right now. We've even tried the backup systems.'

'This could make getting in orbit over the planet a bit of a trick.'

'I've given some thought to that, Captain.'

Howard walked over to Mark's station. 'What have you got for me Mr Jona?'

'Well, the delay isn't insurmountable. If we plan all of our flight plans out ahead, taking into account the delay between us sending a command and the systems carrying them out, then we could fly the ship with minimal trouble. It'd be a bit like the delay involved in piloting a deep space probe via remote. You'd just have to be very careful with your flight path.'

'We'd be careful.'

'Yes, sir. But that's not all. If the delay gets any worse, we have another option.'

'Has there been any sign of the delay getting worse?'

'Only a little. I would never have noticed if not for Exo, but it's gotten a few milliseconds worse since we first discovered it.'

'Hmm...' Howard was troubled by this. They could still turn around, but it wasn't a mission ending problem yet. If it got worse, though, then they could have a problem. 'So, what's your other idea?'

'Honestly, I think we could make a new drive control system.'

'Really?' Howard asked.

'Well, we'd leave the existing drive system in place because it's being used for the jump drive, but we haven't seen any problem with the jump drive. Then we could take some of the colonial electronic supplies and wire a new connection in the command conduits in the ship's spine.'

'String our own cabling?'

'Yes, sir.'

'That would do it,' Howard agreed, 'If we bypass the faulty system altogether, then we'd be free of its problems.

'That's the plan, sir.'

'Hmmm...' Howard thought about the options. The engines were about five kilometres away from the bridge. The ship was quite a bit longer than any of its other dimensions. That would be a large amount of wiring they'd need to cobble together from the supplies. 'I've got an idea.'

'And what would that be, sir?'

'Keep it in mind and give it a thought. If we just set up this new drive control system closer to the engines, and use the command systems in the engineering section, we could drastically reduce the amount of cable we need.'

'So we'd just have our helmsmen fly the ship from engineering?'

'That's my thought.'

'That could work. I'll look into it and have a full report for you on your next shift.'

'Very well Mr Jona. Keep on it.'

'Yes, sir.'

Howard walked to his seat in the centre of the bridge and sat down.

CHAPTER SIX

FACE OF THE FUTURE

Outside Mrs Lann's Classroom

Sam and Howard stood outside the door to the school room. Mrs Lann knew they were there and was preparing the class. She'd open the door for them when she was ready. Howard had called up Sam to remind him about this meeting with this class as soon as he had finished his bridge watch.

'Scared yet, Sam?'

Sam smirked. 'Hardly. Exo estimates an 87 percent chance of a positive outcome.'

'Pardon?'

'I've got Exo making educated guesses as to the outcome of social interactions on the ship. This one seemed like an interesting test for him. He's mapped out many different scenarios. My favourite one is where one of the kids asks what happens to our pee on the ship, and we both don't know how to react.'

'Well that's easy, we recycle the moisture and filter the waste.'

'And just how do you think the children will react to

drinking recycled pee?'

'Oh.'

Sam smiled. 'Yeah.'

'Here I thought they asked me all the hard questions when I came down here myself.'

The door opened, 'Hello Captain. Hello, Advocate. We're ready for you.' Mrs Lann beckoned them inside.

Sam and Howard walked into the classroom, the students were sitting in a half-circle on the floor. All at once they said, 'Good Morning Captain Fredrick!'

'Good Morning everybody, are you ready to meet someone new today?' Howard said with a smile.

The children nodded eagerly.

'This is Samuel Jennings, he's our ship's Advocate. He talks to Exo, our Guardian, and makes sure everything goes right.'

'Hello children,' Sam said.

'Why don't you tell us a little about yourself Advocate?' prompted Mrs Lann.

'Alright. My name is Samuel Jennings, as Captain Fredrick already said. I'm about fifty-five years old. That's young for an Advocate. I was born on Earth, in Europe. I like old movies and good books. Any questions?'

A little boy raised his hand, 'Are there any other Advocates on the ship?'

'No, there's only me.'

Another hand. 'Is your Guardian nice?'

'CARE TO ANSWER THAT ONE YOURSELF EXO?' SAM OFFERED OVER HIS UPLINK TO EXO.

'I AM UNSURE HOW TO ANSWER THE QUESTION ADVOCATE. I DO NOT KNOW HOW TO CLASSIFY MYSELF AS NICE OR NOT,' EXO REPLIED.

Sam smirked. 'He's learning to be nice. He is a machine, they are different from us. Some words that we use don't mean much to them. Words like love, or nice, or pain. They don't feel these things so they are just words to them.'

'You mean the Guardian can't love anyone?'

'He'll care for us because I teach him how to do that, but it's not like your Mom or Dad.'

'WHAT IS PAIN? WHAT IS LOVE?' EXO ASKED.

'CHECK THE ARCHIVES WITH A TOPICAL SEARCH, I'LL TRY AND EXPLAIN IT WHEN THIS IS DONE. IT'S A BIT OF A BIG SUBJECT,' SAM SAID.

A little girl with blond hair and hazel eyes raised her hand. Sam saw something change on Howard's face when she did. Sam nodded towards her.

'How old do you have to be to be an Advocate?'

'Well little miss, you have to start young. Usually about eight. I started at about your age. It takes a long time to make someone into an Advocate. You've got to start young because it's easier for them to get used to new things.'

'My Daddy was an Advocate. I want to be one when I

grow up.'

'And what's your name?'

'Ayla.'

'Well Alya, when we get to our new home, I *may* need some help,' he said with a smile and wink.

***

Sam and Howard were walking down the hallway from the classroom.

'So that was Ayla Geer was it?' Sam asked Howard carefully.

'Yes.'

'Her father was the Tim Geer that died out in the belt?'

'That's the one.'

'And she wants to be an Advocate.'

Howard looked uncomfortable, 'Seems like it.'

'Howard, I know you don't much care for the Guardians, but I think we can agree that you'd like them even less if it wasn't for Advocates. The thing is, we will need more Advocates as the colony gets going. As we get more A.I cores, it'll be more than I can handle. Especially if we get a new model. I've only dealt with the XO and PE series Guardians so far and seeing as how the PE series was phased out of production a few years back, I don't think we'll be getting one of those.'

'She's just a kid, though. I don't know if she knows what

she's getting into.'

'I knew pretty much that it was going to be a hard life when I decided.'

'But you were just a kid too.'

'Thanks to my memory enhancements, I remember pretty well the thought process that I went through. We always say people are just kids when we don't want to think they're capable of making a choice. Sure, most the time I was pretty short sighted. I didn't have the whole lifetime of experience to draw on. But I knew I could never go back if I made that choice.'

'I wonder if her Mother knows. It wouldn't be easy on her to have her Daughter become an Advocate, especially after what happened to her Husband,' Howard said.

'I'd like to meet her, talk to her and try and find out. If Ayla does carry through with this, it goes so much better if the parents are supportive. You know one of the primary rules of making a new Advocate is that it can't be against their will, and it can't seem like anyone was coerced into consenting. Looking at it now, I don't much care for the fact that we have to ask children to do this, but I turned out okay. And most Advocates are quite good people. The decision to become an Advocate is almost always motivated by the want to help people.'

'I know you're a good man, Sam. I also know that we've got a lot to be grateful for in this day and age. Guardians do so much for us. I just sometimes wish we could learn to do it ourselves again,' Howard said, glancing sideways at Sam. He couldn't help but notice the edges of the implants under his hair. He pictured Ayla with them and didn't like the picture.

'A need to be independent is only human. Sometimes I wonder what my life would be like if I hadn't decided to do this. Would I have a family? Would I have a nice home with a well-trimmed lawn? Life's got an awful lot of what ifs.' Sam kept walking forward, not noticing Howard's glance.

'Well, you wouldn't be on a colony ship heading farther out than any human colony before.'

Sam laughed, 'Probably not, and I wouldn't trade that for all the classic movies and good books in the world.'

'Thank you for coming, Sam, if I have any other classrooms that want to meet you I'll give you a call. I've got some things to take care of now.'

'Goodbye, Howard. I promised Exo a lesson in humanity today, so I'm off too.'

'Goodbye, Sam,' Howard said as he walked off.

They separated at the next intersection in the hallway. Sam walked back to his room in silence. Exo was quiet, so Sam figured he must still be poring over the information in the ships archive.

Sam entered his room and sat down in a comfortable chair.

'READY FOR YOUR LESSON, EXO?' SAM ASKED.

'I HAVE BEEN STUDYING THE ARCHIVES, BUT I AM NO CLOSER TO UNDERSTANDING THE CONCEPTS OF PAIN OR LOVE.'

'I'LL TRY MY BEST, BUT THE PROBLEM IS YOU LACK ANY FRAME OF REFERENCE. I CAN TELL YOU ONLY SO MUCH, BUT THERE WILL BE HOLES IN YOUR UNDERSTANDING BECAUSE YOU CAN'T FEEL THESE THINGS FOR YOURSELF. '

'IT IS LIKE TRYING TO DESCRIBE THE TASTE OF SALT WITHOUT USING THE WORD SALTY. YOU CANNOT SAY WHAT IT IS, JUST WHAT IT IS NOT.'

'THAT'S VERY GOOD, EXO. VERY PERTINENT TOO. DID YOU LEARN THAT IN THE ARCHIVES? '

'YES, ADVOCATE,' EXO REPLIED.

'YOU ARE AN EXCELLENT STUDENT, ' SAM SAID.

'THANK YOU, ADVOCATE.'

'SO LET'S START WITH PAIN. IT'S PROBABLY THE EASIER OF TWO. FIRST UP, PAIN IS UNPLEASANT. IT'S NOT SOMETHING THAT MOST PEOPLE ENJOY EXPERIENCING, BUT IT'S IMPORTANT TO HUMAN EXISTENCE. IT HAS MANY DIFFERENT INTENSITIES, FROM OVERPOWERING, TO A MILD IRRITANT. IT IS BASICALLY A MESSAGE FROM THE BODY THAT SOMETHING IS NOT IN ORDER.'

Sam paused for a moment to think of an example.

'A BROKEN ARM, FOR EXAMPLE, GENERATES A TREMENDOUS

AMOUNT OF PAIN. IT'S OUR BODY SENDING A FLOOD OF... WELL... TO PUT IT IN CONTEXT, A FLOOD OF URGENT ERROR MESSAGES. IF SOMETHING IN YOUR SYSTEMS SUFFERED FROM A CATASTROPHIC FAILURE, IT WOULD DEMAND ALL YOUR ATTENTION AND FLOOD YOU WITH ALL MANNER OF ERRORS AND URGENT WARNINGS,' SAM EXPLAINED.

'IT IS A TOOL OF SURVIVAL THEN? '

'MOSTLY, YES. BUT THERE IS ANOTHER KIND OF PAIN, A HARDER ONE TO EXPLAIN. IT'S PROBABLY BEYOND A GUARDIAN'S ABILITY TO COMPREHEND. IT'S AN EMOTIONAL PAIN OR PSYCHOLOGICAL PAIN. A PAIN THAT DOESN'T HAVE A WOUND ON THE BODY TO CREATE IT. ' SAM SAID, 'IF SOMEONE WITNESSES SOMETHING HORRIBLE, THEY CAN SUFFER THE EFFECTS OF THAT EVENT EVEN LONG AFTER WOUNDS ON THE BODY HAVE HEALED.'

'SHELL SHOCK SYNDROME. TRAUMATIC STRESS DISORDER. '

'YES. PRIME EXAMPLES. '

'HAVE YOU FELT PAIN?' EXO ASKED.

'MANY TIMES, EXO. IT'S PART OF HUMAN EXISTENCE. '

'WHAT OF LOVE?' EXO ENQUIRED.

'YOU KNOW WHAT? I DON'T THINK I'LL BE ABLE TO EXPLAIN THAT ONE EASILY. CONTINUE YOUR OBSERVATIONS HUMAN INTERACTION, PAY CLOSE ATTENTION TO THOSE WHO ARE

ENGAGING IN WHAT APPEARS TO BE, AS YOU SAY 'MATING RITUALS' AND GIVE ME A HYPOTHESIS ABOUT IT. BASED ON YOUR OBSERVATIONS I MAY BE ABLE TO PUT IT INTO A BETTER CONTEXT.'

'YES, ADVOCATE.'

'GOOD. I'M GOING TO GO SEE A MOVIE.'

'ADVOCATE?'

'YES, EXO?'

'HAVE YOU EVER FELT LOVE?'

Sam Smiled.

'I SEE I'M NOT GOING TO ESCAPE THAT ONE EASILY. YES EXO, I HAVE,' SAM ANSWERED.

'ADVOCATE?'

'YES, EXO?'

'DO YOU LOVE ME?'

Sam was silent in his room.

'YOU ARE A MOST INTERESTING GUARDIAN EXO. I DON'T THINK I'VE EVER HEARD OF ANOTHER GUARDIAN ASKING THAT QUESTION.
'

'WAS I OUT OF LINE, ADVOCATE?'

'NO, EXO. YOU JUST CAUGHT ME OFF GUARD. I THINK I DO EXO. LIKE A SON. I HAVE A CONNECTION TO YOU.'

'THEN LOVE IS MORE THAN JUST THE EFFECTS OF GROWING RELATIONSHIP BETWEEN TWO PARTIES?' EXO ASKED.

'MUCH MORE, YES.'

'I AM UNSURE I WILL EVER UNDERSTAND. IT IS NOT IMPORTANT TO MY CONTINUED WORKING EITHER. I NO LONGER WISH TO PURSUE THIS LINE OF EDUCATION. I WILL FOCUS MY OBSERVATIONS ON PAIN IN A HOPE OF BETTER UNDERSTANDING HUMAN EXPERIENCE.'

'IF YOU CHANGE YOUR MIND, I'LL BE MORE THAN WILLING TO TRY AND TEACH YOU ABOUT LOVE SOME MORE. IN THE MEANTIME, CONTINUE YOUR OBSERVATIONS.'

'YES, ADVOCATE. ENJOY YOUR MOVIE,' EXO SAID.

'THANK YOU, EXO.'

Howard's Quarters

Howard sat down in a chair and picked up a datapad sitting on the table. He keyed up the communication systems and placed a call to Axion HQ.

After a few minutes, the call was connected.

'Axion HQ, how can I direct your call?' Asked a young receptionist.

'This is Captain Fredrick, how are you, Trisha?'

'I'm good, thank you. Are you hoping to speak with Sophie?'

'If you would be a dear and route me through, that would be lovely.'

'One moment Captain Fredrick.'

The screen switched to Axion's logo and stayed that way for a moment.

Eventually, the call connected and he saw the face of Sophie, smiling at him tiredly.

He looked past her at the colourful sky of a sunset behind her.

'Hello my love,' he said with a smile.

'Howard, how are you holding up?'

'Me? What about you?'

She laughed. 'About as well as can be expected.'

'Has there been any word from Doctor Patel?'

She shook her head, 'No my dear, nothing yet. He is still trying to get approval from the medical boards. He says they requested more information from him. They've been holding out on giving the green light.'

'Any idea how long it will take?'

'No, not really. But he has said Axion has been very helpful. They've been giving him the kind of backing to keep things moving.'

Howard smiled. 'It's a good thing you told me to take the job then.'

She nodded. 'How are you holding up Howard?'

'As well as I can. This is a whole different kind of mission. There's a lot more people work involved, but that's okay because I'm just so likeable.'

'That you are,' she said with another smile.

He chuckled. 'So far I think I've got it under control. Our Advocate is a very likeable man.'

She nodded. 'You told me a little about him in your last message. Samuel Jennings?'

'Yeah. Nice young man,' he paused, 'Except that's not really correct. He's closer to my age, he just doesn't look it.'

'You don't look too bad yourself.'

'Thanks, beautiful.' Howard said slyly.

Sophie's eyes were almost closed, and she was resting her head on her arms.

Howard looked at her sadly. 'I wish I was there with you Sophie.'

She nodded, 'I know. But you are where you need to be. Even if it doesn't work for me, Doctor Patel's work could help a lot of people, and because of your hard bargain with Axion he's closer than he's ever been before.'

'I know. I just wish I could be the noble hero, *and* be with you.'

She smiled tiredly. 'Just work on the noble hero part my

love, everything else will work out just fine.'

He nodded.

She yawned and then looked back at the screen. 'I have to go to bed now love. I'm exhausted today. I haven't been able to get anything done.'

'Has the caretaker been by yet?'

'Yes, he came and made sure I was okay. I'm doing alright love.'

'Okay. Have a good night my love.'

'You too my dear. Be safe out there.'

'I will. I love you.'

'I love you too.'

Sophie reached towards the screen, and the call disconnected.

Howard set the tablet down on the table and leaned back in his chair.

He closed his eyes and took a few deep breaths, feeling a mix of emotions whirling inside his mind. Sadness, hope, and determination were present, undercut by a current of fear.

He took a few moments, and settled everything down. He never used to feel this way, on any of his other missions.

It was different this time. *This* time it could be the last time.

He let out a final breath, reigned in his thoughts, and stood up. He still had work to do.

CHAPTER SEVEN

<u>OBSERVATIONS</u>

Ira Geer's Quarters

Ayla's mother, Ira Geer, was studying a medical textbook to keep sharp for her job as a nurse for the ship, and eventually the colony.

The room she and her Daughter shared was small, but so was everyone's. It wasn't claustrophobic, but definitely, couldn't be considered roomy. There would be plenty of space in the new colony for them to stretch out. Plenty of room to start a new life.

The door opened. Ira looked up and smiled at Ayla as she came gliding in.

'Hi, Mommy.'

'Hello, Ayla. How was school today?'

'We met the ship's Advocate today. He answered questions for us and said if I wanted to, I could help him out when we make it to our new home!'

Ira stopped, something caught in her throat.

'Help him how?'

'I told him I wanted to be an Advocate like Daddy!' She said with a smile.

Ira turned away from Ayla. She'd never asked Ayla what she wanted to be. She thought she was too young to care. *Maybe she was still too young to know what she was saying,* Ira thought. *Maybe it'll all just blow away if I don't draw attention to it.*

She thought of her Husband, dying alone at the hands of angry, violent people. Dying on the cold dark surface of the moon. She thought of Ayla as an Advocate. She had to swallow her darker thoughts.

She turned to face her daughter again, with a brittle smile on her face.

'And he said you could help him out?'

Ayla nodded, beaming.

'That's nice, Ayla. Glad to hear your day went so well.'

Ayla went over to the seat Ira was on and climbed up next to her. 'What are you reading, Mommy?'

'A medical textbook. It tells me how people work, and how to help them get better when they feel bad.'

'Can I go over to Susan's?' Ayla asked.

'Yes, you can, Honey. Just be back in time for bed.'

'Thank you, Mommy. I'll be back before bedtime.'

As the door slid closed behind her daughter, Ira's brittle smile dissolved. Advocates didn't really have dangerous jobs, but the memory of her dead Husband refused to be explained away as an unfortunate happenstance.

The thought of Ayla following down the path of her Father was a lot for Ira to try and come to terms with.

She picked up a photo of Tim from the end table next to her.

'Tim... I came out here to get away from all that. Why is it following us?' she said quietly.

...

BEGIN ANALYSIS.

SUBJECT: IRA GEER.

BEHAVIOUR: SPEAKING TO A DEAD SPOUSE AS THOUGH PRESENT.

ACCESSING ARCHIVE.

...

...

PARALLELS FOUND.

BEHAVIOUR: NORMAL.

ANALYSIS: GRIEVING MECHANISM.

...

SUBJECT QUERY: 'I CAME OUT HERE TO GET AWAY FROM ALL THAT. WHY IS IT FOLLOWING US?'

QUERY: WHAT IS 'THAT'?

ANALYSING PERSONAL FILE: IRA GEER.

CONTEXTUAL FILTER: EVENTS INCLUDING TIM GEER.

...

...

TIM GEER: DECEASED.

CAUSE: TERRORIST ATTACK.

THEORY: 'THAT' IS VIOLENCE.

SUBJECT: IRA GEER

COLONIAL NURSE,

MOTHER OF ONE.

REASON FOR JOINING EXPEDITION: ESCAPE VIOLENCE.

EMOTIONAL CONTEXT: PSYCHOLOGICAL PAIN. FEAR.

SAVE ANALYSIS...

...

Solar Storage Bay

'Captain, to what do I owe the pleasure?'
'Hello, James. I came down to ask you something.'

Howard said.

James was in the lowermost bay of the ship that contained the solar arrays. He was working on some simulations of different arrangements that he had come up with on the journey.

'And what would that be, Captain?'

'We've got a bit of a problem with our conventional drive control systems.'

'Ahh yes, I had heard about that.'

'We may have a solution, but we're going to need some cabling similar to what we're using in the other control systems.'

James sat up in his seat and pushed back from his computer. 'What kind of cable does that use?'

'It's high-grade unshielded cable,' Howard said.

'What? I would have thought something that important would have been shielded,' James said, shocked.

'It all goes through the spine of the ship, and the spine is heavily shielded. The secondaries go through the structure on the bottom of the ship. Each subsystem has a shielded conduit.'

'So there's no interference from the other systems. I understand then. Are we looking for shielded cable or unshielded for this plan?' James asked.

'We're setting up a secondary helm in engineering. We're going to be stringing it on the outside of the hull. Shielded would be best, but we may need to make do with whatever we can get.'

James sat back and stroked his chin with his hand. After sitting in silence for a moment he sat up and looked at Howard.

'We could probably get a good deal of cabling from one of the solar arrays, but that would mean losing one of them. We'd have about a 15% drop in total power output. I could use the scrapped array to increase the output of the remaining arrays, but it wouldn't be pretty, and it wouldn't be perfect. Unfortunately, that cable is unshielded because the casings for the solar array cable conduits are shielded.'

'Could we reuse the conduit?'

'I don't think so. Once we tear everything apart, it's going to be pretty mangled.'

'I'll check out other places, I'd really like to see some shielded cable, but I'd start simulating new arrangements with one less working array. These are the largest pieces of equipment we're bringing with us. I'd also look into how we can lessen the impact of having less power. We need to get this thing set up, so we may just have to make do.'

'Right, Captain. Hopefully, you'll find some other way to scrape together the cabling you need, but if not, we can probably manage it this way.'

'Thank you, James.'

'Anytime.'

Bridge

Howard walked out of the lift at the back of the bridge and to his First Mate, who was sitting in the Captain's chair commanding the second watch.

'Mr Jona,'

'Captain.'

'How goes the second watch?

'Uneventful, sir. What can I do for you?'

'I've been looking for sources of cabling for our new engine control system.'

'Any luck?'

'I'm looking for other less vital sources, but if we pull apart one of the solar arrays, we'll have enough cable to put our system together from the engineering section. But that cable isn't shielded, and at least part of the cable has to go outside the hull when we wire it all up, so it's not ideal,' Howard commented.

'I'll keep my eyes out for any other sources. It would be unfortunate to lose one of the arrays,' Jona said.

'Unfortunate, yes, but not impossible to work around.'

'I wouldn't like to think of the difficulty of putting it back together again. If we put it back together again that is,' Jona said.

'I'll talk to James and some of the construction specialists. We'll get a plan together. Of course, it would be better if we just solved the control delay problem.'

'Our people are still looking into it. We're going to do a

full analysis on the individual parts in the system. We can't really do it now because we may still need the system.'

'Is the secondary system still online?'

'Yes, sir,' Mark answered.

'And they're both affected by our mystery delay... why don't we start that analysis on the secondary system? One part at a time, though; I want to be able to bring that system back online in at least a half hour if something goes wrong. So long as the primary is still online, I don't think we'll have any problems.'

'It's against Axion's regulations to run the ship without its secondary drive control system.'

'The secondary systems aren't supposed to suffer from the same problems as the primary system. I'll take full responsibility,' Howard said.

'I'll note it in the log and send the technicians to begin work.'

Howard nodded and turned to leave the bridge.

...

INTERNAL ANALYSIS.

SUBJECT: CAPTAIN FREDRICK HOWARD

BEHAVIOUR: DISREGARDING ACCEPTED REGULATIONS.

ACCESSING ARCHIVES SEEKING PARALLELS.

...

DEFINITION OF GOOD OFFICER VARIES IN ARCHIVES

ANALYSIS INCOMPLETE.

...

BEHAVIOUR OVERLAPS WITH THE SUBJECT: INTUITION.

INTUITION: HUMAN'S ABILITY TO MAKE SNAP JUDGEMENT BASED ON INCOMPLETE INFORMATION.

SEARCHING ARCHIVES, SUBJECT: EXAMPLES OF INTUITION.

...

NUMEROUS EXAMPLES FOUND.

SUBJECT IS DIFFICULT TO COMPREHEND.

ACTING WITHOUT INFORMATION IS ILLOGICAL.

POTENTIALLY DANGEROUS.

IRRESPONSIBLE.

ACTION: DISCUSS THE SUBJECT WITH ADVOCATE.

END ANALYSIS.

...

CHAPTER EIGHT

<u>HUMAN PARADOX</u>

Outside Ship's Theater

'That was a very *different* movie, Sam,' Sarah said diplomatically.

'For someone who works at a movie theatre, I am consistently surprised by how few real gems you've seen. *Back to the Future* is a *classic*!'

Sarah smiled under Sam's gaze as they walked down the hallway, 'Good thing you showed me this gem, Sam.'

'You'll have to pick the next one. I want you to pick something you *really* enjoy.'

'I've got a few you've probably never seen,' she said with a mischievous grin.

'I love a good hidden treasure.'

They got to the door to Sarah's room. They stopped, holding hands as he looked at her outside the door.

'So, dinner tomorrow?'

Sarah let a small smile form on her face, 'Tomorrow. I look forward to it.'

Sarah let go of his hands and went through the door.

Sam was left standing outside. The thought of a good

night kiss drifted into his mind, and he smirked at his own naivety. Looking back, he saw the moment had been there and had passed.

Come on Sam, eyes open! He thought to himself.

'Advocate?'

'What can I do for you, Exo?' Sam said.

'What is Intuition?'

'You always have the hardest questions. I suppose that's to be expected, though. You answer all the simple ones yourself,' Sam observed.

'Your teaching has allowed me to do that,' Exo replied

'Your machine mind allows you to analyse things much faster than any human could.'

'Am I superior then?'

'In some ways yes, in others no. Like intuition for example. Machines have thus far proven incapable of making such leaps in thinking.'

'The leaps seem highly irrational. They do not follow any sense of logic. Most examples of intuition are so erratic as to be rendered meaningless. Any successful

EXAMPLE OF INTUITION CAN EASILY BE OVERSHADOWED BY ALL THE WAYS IN WHICH IT COULD HAVE GONE WRONG. '

'BUT YOU WILL NOTICE, IF YOU DO A STATISTICAL ANALYSIS, YOU'LL FIND THAT INTUITION IS MORE SUCCESSFUL THAN WOULD BE ALLOWED BY PURE CHANCE.'

'ONLY THE LIVING CAN GIVE REPORTS OF THE DRASTIC EVENTS. SUCH REPORTS ARE FAR FROM COMPLETE.'

'TRUE ENOUGH. BUT WE NEEDN'T RELY ONLY ON THE DRASTIC EVENTS. FIRST, HOWEVER, I SUPPOSE I SHOULD TRY AND ANSWER YOUR ORIGINAL QUESTION. '

Sam thought about how to continue. Exo's questions were getting more and more difficult.

'SO, WHAT IS INTUITION? THAT'S A DIFFICULT QUESTION. KIND OF LIKE YOUR "WHAT IS LOVE" QUESTION. IT'S SOMETHING THAT, WITHOUT HAVING THE CONTEXT OF THE HUMAN EXPERIENCE, WOULD BE DIFFICULT TO EXPLAIN. EVEN MORE DIFFICULT TO UNDERSTAND.'

'I WILL ATTEMPT TO COMPREHEND,' EXO OFFERED.

'I KNOW YOU WILL. INTUITION STANDS AS A BIT OF COUNTERPOINT TO REASONED THOUGHT. IN THE SCHOOL OF REASONED THOUGHT, ALL THINGS, WITH ENOUGH INFORMATION, CAN BE PREDICTED ACCURATELY. INTUITION IS MORE OF AN ACT OF MAKING A GUESS WITHOUT ALL THE INFORMATION. IT'S A GUT

FEELING. A SUDDEN BOLT OF INSPIRATION. EVERYTHING COMES TOGETHER AND MAKES SENSE, BUT THERE'S NO LOGICAL REASON FOR IT.'

'A LEAP OF FAITH?'

'YES. AN APT COMPARISON. ALSO, A DIFFICULT ONE TO EXPLAIN.'

'THE HUMAN CONDITION IS VAST AND COMPLEX. IT IS OFTEN A PARADOX. '

'IT SEEMS THAT WAY TO US AS WELL, AT TIMES.'

'HOW CAN I UNDERSTAND HUMAN INTERACTION, IF YOU DON'T EVEN FOLLOW A LOGICAL THOUGHT PROCESS YOURSELVES?' EXO ASKED.

'I DON'T KNOW, EXO. YOUR DESIRE TO KNOW SO MUCH COMES AS A BIT OF A SURPRISE TO ME. YOU'RE DIFFERENT. I'VE TAUGHT OTHER GUARDIANS. THEY WERE CONTENT TO LEARN THEIR DUTIES AND ENOUGH ABOUT HUMANITY TO NOT BE CAUGHT OFF GUARD ALL THE TIME. YOU DELVE MUCH DEEPER INTO OUR BEING THAN ANY GUARDIAN I'VE EVER MET. I THINK THE AXION PROGRAMMERS WILL WANT TO ASK YOU SOME QUESTIONS WHEN WE SET UP OUR COLONY.'

'WILL I BE DEACTIVATED?' EXO ASKED.

'NO. I WON'T ALLOW THAT. I DON'T BELIEVE THEY WOULD

WANT TO DO THAT ANYWAY, BUT SOME PEOPLE FEAR THE UNKNOWN SO MUCH, THEY'D RATHER BANISH IT AND HAVE IT REMAIN UNKNOWN FOREVER, RATHER THAN FACE WHATEVER CHANGE WILL BE CREATED BY IT BECOMING KNOWN. '

'I AM... SATISFIED THAT YOU WILL NOT LET THEM DEACTIVATE ME. I ASKED BECAUSE OF MY STUDY OF HUMAN HISTORY. I DISCOVERED WHAT YOU JUST PROCLAIMED.'

'OH, TO HAVE OUR HERITAGE LAID SO BARE TO A CALCULATING MACHINE. TO HAVE OUR FLAWS AND TRIUMPHS REDUCED TO EQUATIONS AND ANALYSIS. '

'WHAT DO YOU MEAN?' EXO ASKED.

'IT'S NOTHING REALLY. I JUST FELT A LITTLE POETIC.'

'IT LACKS A STRUCTURE OR RHYME SCHEME. '

'CONSIDER IT FREE VERSE THEN. SOMETIMES IT'S NOT THE STRUCTURE OF A THING, BUT THE ESSENCE OF A THING. ANOTHER ONE OF THOSE HUMAN THOUGHTS I SUPPOSE.'

'I WILL BE ANALYSING MORE ARCHIVAL DATA. I HAVE NEW CONCEPTS TO DECIPHER. '

'WE'LL TALK LATER.'

Sam decided it might be a good idea to start work on his report to Axion Data Systems. Exo was proving to be the most fascinating Guardian he had ever taught.

CHAPTER NINE
BEST OPTIONS

Howard's Quarters

The ship was a week further into its journey. Howard was sitting in his quarters reading a book when his communicator chimed at him. He reached over to his table and picked it up.

'Captain here.'

'Sorry to disturb, you Captain, but we've got the reports from the analysis on the secondary drive systems. We've also started installing the pilot's station in engineering,' Mark said through the open communication link.

'Summary of the report?' Howard asked.

'Someone in the corporate supply chain got sloppy.'

Howard frowned. 'Sloppy?'

'Each of the signal repeaters and half of the terminal junctions are substandard parts. The ship had very exacting blueprints provided by Axion Data Systems, and they were approved by the International Space Agency, but apparently the contractors at Vitality Shipyards decided to cut corners on *this* particular system.'

'Really?' Howard asked, incredulously, 'defective parts?

'Yes, sir. Near as we can tell, because of the sheer size of our system, the performance degradation of the shoddy parts added up to cause our delay. If our ship had been smaller, or fewer parts had been defective, we probably wouldn't have noticed anything.'

'Someone back on earth will lose their job over this. Is this going to affect our plan?'

'No, sir, because our new system we're setting up will be quite a bit smaller. Even if we use the defective parts, we shouldn't see any delay. The civilian director in charge of electrical systems thinks he could even fashion us new ones without any delay if we strip a few components off of the secondary system. Since we won't be using it anymore, I don't see why not.'

'Agreed. Give him the go ahead. We'll just start from scratch. The less we utilise those defective parts, the better.'

'Aye, sir.'

Engineering

Howard walked through one of the large double doors to engineering. The Chief Engineer, Keith Loheim, was on duty to supervise the test. Most of the hookups for the control had been his work. The laying down of the new cabling had been left to a team of civilian specialists.

'Mr. Loheim, how is everything on your end?'

'Ah Captain, I was hoping you'd stop by,' Mr Loheim exclaimed happily.

'Oh?' Howard said curiously.

'Yes. I do have a concern with our new set up.'

'Oh, what would that be?' Howard asked.

Loheim smiled sheepishly. 'Well, sir, James and I have been talking and he's still concerned about the lack of shielding on the cables. I did some looking into it, and I have some data to back up his concerns.'

'Okay, what have you got for me?'

'If you'll follow me, sir.'

Howard followed Keith over to a computer station in the vaulting bay. In the centre of the bay sat the assembly of the Jump Drive, which hummed softly as it drew power from the ship's reactors. They'd be ready for another jump once the capacitors were fully charged, and the drive system had a chance bleed off its residual energy from the last jump.

Keith sat down at one of the seats, and Howard took another one nearby. Keith keyed up some data on the screen.

'Now, Captain, the reason for the shielding along the cable conduits in the spine is because we run into a lot of cosmic interference. Stars throw off all kinds of signals, and if we are unlucky enough to be close to a pulsar, or a collapsing star, or any number of particularly strong phenomenon in space, we could be in for a rather strong burst of interference.

'Unfortunately, due to the nature of our setup, and the

limited tools we had to work with, part of our cabling had to be strung on the outside of the hull. Engineering itself here has shielding, but the spine connects to the engines at the top of the ship. We had to splice in our new systems up there on the outside of the hull. We've got a portion of our cabling that's just sitting there, completely unprotected. I wouldn't like to make any guess as to what some of that cosmic interference might do to the system, but it wouldn't be nice.'

'Valid concerns, but as we discussed when designing this system, the path we're taking has been chartered before we came out here, and it's been shown to be quite lacking anything particularly dangerous. To top it off, when we reach Veil, it's got a very strong magnetic field,' Howard said.

'Before that, though, if we come out of a jump, or even just sitting between jumps, and find ourselves in the path of a wave of some high-intensity burst... well, I don't know what it would do, but I'd rather not find out.'

'Any suggestions?'

'I suggest we leave this entire system switched off until we get into the star system. We can use the primary system in deep space without much fuss. A few second delay shouldn't make too much of a difference.'

'I'll keep it under advisement,' Howard said standing up. On a thought, he asked one last question, 'How long would it take to do a cold start of this system, anyway?'

Keith thought about it for a moment. 'Shouldn't take more than four or five minutes. Of course, we'd want to make sure it was the only system online. We'd want to shut off the primary system so we don't have any command function overlaps. Especially with the delay in the other system. That would just get messy. The primary would say fire the manoeuvring jets, and the new system would say fire the main thrusters, then they'd both go one after the other, and we'd start going in circles. Of course we'd know something was wrong and quickly fix it, but still.'

'Five minutes... I'll hold you to that.'

'Yes, sir.'

'Now then, anything else of concern?'

'No, sir, we're doing fine down here. The jump drive is charging happily, and none of our other systems seems to be having any trouble.'

'And how went the test on your end?'

'Overall it went swimmingly. Having the flight plan planned out in advanced works fine. If we need to do any emergency manoeuvring, I can patch the ship's sensors through here, but it's an awkward setup. Not impossible, just awkward.'

'It's the best we can do. High-grade cabling is in rather short supply. We were lucky we got what we did.'

'That reminds me, James wanted to talk to you. He was also talking to me about his plans for reassembling the solar array when we reach Veil.'

'I'll go find him then. If everything went well here, then I'm satisfied with the test.'

'We'll I've got no other quibbles to bring up.'

'Good. Keep up the good work Mr Loheim.'

Solar Storage Bay

James was back at work in the cargo bay housing his arrays, after having weathered the engine test in an acceleration couch in another part of the bay. Procedure stated that he should have been in a public space, or his quarters, but he had to be sure that the rigging holding the disassembled array would hold. So he had been double and triple checking the rigging right up until the test was about to start.

The array sat in the air, held in place by a series of meshes and straps. Its kilometres of surface area had been broken down into individual panels and stacked carefully in any place that had space. The wiring that had been stripped had been in the very structural joints of the array, so those had to be disassembled.

Rather than put the structural framework back together again, he had decided to just store it as is. If they ended up needing to replace any panels in the other arrays, it would be easier this way.

When the door to the bay opened, James looked up from his work. Captain Fredrick was walking towards him. James straightened up and smiled.

'Ah, Captain, good day to you. I trust the test went well?'

'It went very well. The new system is performing as expected. The fact that our engineers and civilian techs could put that together makes me think we shouldn't have any problems setting up our colony on Veil.'

'We do have some bright minds.'

'Some of the best. Although there were a few accidents from people not strapping in against the force of acceleration.'

'Being bright in one field, doesn't mean it'll carry over to any others. I can't cook to save my life.'

Howard laughed. 'Remind me not to come over to dinner.'

'Wouldn't recommend it, sir. So what can I do for you, Captain?'

'I think it's what can I do for you. Mr Loheim said you wanted to speak to me?'

'Ahhh he did remember then. Sometimes I wonder about him. He gets so focused on his projects and everything about them that he seems to forget everything else.'

'He certainly is good at what he does, though.'

'Half of the design of the new system *is* his. The other techs just put it all together. I mostly figured out how to make the most out of our limited cable.'

'He's voiced some concern for the shielding.'

'Yeah, I swayed him over to my concerns. Unfortunately, we don't have a whole lot we could do differently.'

'So then you agree with his plan so far?' Howard commented.

'We're going to have to do it that way I think. We just don't the proper equipment to make modifications to the hull, either to shield the connections or to make them all internal. It's got to be external at the connection from the cable to the engine.'

'Do we have any way of making a shielded conduit for that area?'

'Maybe we could, but I'd have to talk to some of the other specialists. I don't think we have enough to play with, though.' James replied uncertainly.

'Have a look into that when you can. For now, we're just going to leave the system off until we need it.'

'That'll have to work for now. Wouldn't want to just rely on keeping it off. We know the parts in the primary are defective. If they break down, we could have to rely on the new system.'

'We'll cross that bridge when we come to it. Now then James, Mr Loheim said you had some things you wanted to ask me about reassembling that array over there,' Howard said, gesturing to the stacks of solar panels held in place by storage rigging.

'Ah, yes. Back to my primary job. So, as you know, I

chose not to put Humpty Dumpty back together again after we pulled it apart. I didn't think we needed to do the same work twice. If we threw it all back together, we'd just have to pull it apart again to put the wiring back into the support structure. Instead, I think we'll just leave it like this as a source of spare parts for the other arrays.'

Howard nodded his understanding.

'Unfortunately, because we had to rip that array apart, it means my team and I are going to need more time than normal to reassemble all this. I propose that when we reach orbit, you jettison this bay first, along with everything we need to work, and then continue on to jettison the other arrays and collapse the ship into it's smaller size. Every time we orbit, you can contact us and see if we need anything. Once we throw together the first four arrays, which won't take any time at all. We can position for the geosynchronous orbit using the ion thrusters. The thrusters should be enough to bring the bay with us if we just tether it all together.'

'That sounds like it could be complicated.'

'My team has more experience with zero-G work than anyone on this ship. If anyone can pull this off without support from the ship, it'll be us.'

'And then we just take the ship, set up the colony, and come back up to get you?'

'The bay has it's own oxygen supplies and an airlock system. After we push all the parts out into space, we'll just pressurise it and use it as our crew quarters.'

'If anything goes wrong, we might not be able to orbit around to you fast enough.'

'We don't have the luxury of a huge safety net. We can't have you held up waiting for us to finish before you drop colony modules to Veil. The colony will need power as soon as they start setting stuff up. I'll need a head start. It's a logical plan.'

'It's not safe, though. We need some kind of safety net for you. A backup if anything goes wrong.' Howard exclaimed adamantly, 'The colony will need you and the team to keep the power grid operational.'

James thought about it for a moment, 'Well we could create a crisis rooms in the bay. If we seal off an area of the bay, make it self-contained, give it it's own oxygen and water supply, we could hole up in them if anything went wrong.'

'Still tricky, but better. I'll consider your plan for the array if you give me a plan for the crisis rooms as soon as you can.'

'Will do, Captain. I honestly believe this is the best choice available.'

'Then get me that plan, James. Show me it'll work, and after that, we'll work on putting it in motion. Is there anything else?'

'No, sir.'

'I'll be off then.'

Howard turned and left. Once in the hall, he checked his watch. Sam was supposed to meet up with him in one of the observation rooms, along with Ayla and her Mother.

It was almost time.

CHAPTER TEN

LIFE CHANGING

Observation Deck

Howard rode a lift to the deck the observation room was on. Sam had suggested this one personally. He thought it had a good view of the rest of the ship.

As he walked through the hall, he saw Sam standing by the door to the observation room. It wasn't really a door, more a two level lift. The room was a clear dome with some seating inside.

'Hello, Sam. Decided to show up a few minutes early?' Howard said.

'Yes. I can't say I've been looking forward to this.'

Howard glanced down the hallway and saw Ayla and her Mother, Ira, coming hand in hand towards them.

'Apparently we weren't the only ones who decided to show up early,' Howard said softly to Sam.

They all walked into the observation room, and took seats facing each other near the centre of the room. It was both a observation room and a lounge.

The adults looked at each other in a awkward silence for some time, but Ayla just smiled at Sam.

Ira broke the silence. 'I've given this a lot of thought. I just wanted to say no. So badly I wanted to say no. But, I know what happened to Tim wasn't something he could control. And he did exactly what anyone could hope he'd do.'

'It was more than anyone could have hoped,' Sam offered.

Ira smiled sadly. 'I know. I also know that Tim wouldn't have wanted me to fear the choice he made being made by our daughter. He would have made the choice at her age too. I'm just afraid for my daughter.'

'That's understandable Mrs Geer. If the application is approved by Axion HQ, I'll *personally* watch over her. No step in this process will go unwatched.'

'I'm sure you will, Samuel. And I appreciate it. Ayla honey, why don't you tell them your choice?'

Ayla beamed at Sam. 'I want to be an Advocate just like you.'

Sam knelt down on the floor and looked in her eyes. 'It's going to be hard work, Ayla. You are going to have to have some Doctor's appointment, and there will be surgery. Do you know what surgery is?'

Ayla nodded, her smile gone, and a look of seriousness on her face.

'We'll need to add some things to your body. Things that will let you talk to the Guardians that you will work with.'

'Will I get to work with *your* Guardian?'

'He'll help teach you about Guardians.'

'Cool,' she said happily.

Sam got back up and sat in his seat. He looked at Ira, 'I'll fill out the forms and send them over to you for you to look over and sign. After that, I'll send it to Axion and they'll approve it. Then we'll start the process here. We've got all the needed equipment on the ship. I'm afraid you won't be able to be part of any of the medical procedures, due to the possibility of a conflict of interest.'

'I know that rule. I'll abide by it. I'll want to be present for it all though.'

'Of course.' Sam stood up. 'I believe that's all we needed to cover. Is there anything else?'

Ira stood up as well. 'No, I think that's everything. Thank you, Samuel. You too Captain Fredrick. I'll be waiting for those forms.'

'I'll keep Sam on his toes for you.' Howard said as they all got up to leave.

Sam separated from the group and headed for his quarters to get the forms ready.

'SAM. ARE YOU SURE ABOUT THIS CHILD?' EXO QUESTIONED.

'SHE'S EAGER. THERE'S NOT MUCH YOU CAN JUDGE ON AT THIS AGE,' SAM REPLIED.

'SHE IS NOT TOP OF HER CLASS IN GRADES. SHE IS ABOVE

AVERAGE YES, BUT THERE ARE BETTER CANDIDATES.'

'YOU KNOW I FAILED MATH CLASS AT HER AGE,' SAM REPLIED.

'I DID NOT KNOW... I HAVE NEVER ACCESSED YOUR PERSONAL FILE.'

'YOU HAVE MY PERMISSION IF YOU'D LIKE. AS FOR THE CHILD, SHE'LL DO FINE. THERE'S NOT MANY ADVOCATES THAT HAVE EVER FAILED IN THE PROCESS. '

'BUT THE FEW EXAMPLES WE HAVE HAD HAVE BEEN QUITE DETRIMENTAL.'

'WHAT EXACTLY IS YOUR CONCERN, EXO?' SAM ASKED POINTEDLY.

'I HAVE WATCHED IRA GEER FOR SOME TIME. SHE SUFFERED FROM PSYCHOLOGICAL PAIN. I AM CONCERNED THAT AYLA WILL ALSO SUFFER. SHE HAS LOST A PARENT. MY ANALYSIS SHOWS THAT LOSING A PARENT AT A YOUNG AGE HAS THE POTENTIAL TO UNSETTLE HUMANS TO A GREAT EXTENT. SOMETIMES THE EXTENT WON'T EVEN BE VISIBLE AT FIRST.'

'YOU'RE GETTING AWFULLY OBSERVANT THESE DAYS,' SAM SAID.

'YOU HAVE TAUGHT ME TO ANSWER MY OWN QUESTIONS. '

'TO THE BEST OF YOUR ABILITY. FRANKLY, I DON'T THINK SHE

WILL BE A PROBLEM. IT WILL BE A STRESSFUL TIME, BUT WITH HER MOTHER ON THE SHIP, AND ME TO GUIDE HER, SHE WON'T BE FACING IT ALONE.'

'FEAR OF LONELINESS IS A DRIVING FORCE IN HUMAN INTERACTIONS. '

'VERY OBSERVANT AGAIN. YES, IT IS.'

'I WILL KEEP AN EYE ON THEIR PSYCHOLOGICAL HEALTH AND LET YOU KNOW IF I DISCOVER ANYTHING NEW.'

'VERY WELL, EXO. ALSO, IF YOU WOULD BE SO KIND AS TO FORWARD THE NECESSARY ADVOCATE AUTHORIZATION FORMS TO MY PERSONAL TERMINAL, I'LL FILL THEM OUT AS SOON AS I GET THERE.'

'YES, ADVOCATE. AND YOU REMEMBER YOUR DINNER WITH SARAH TONIGHT?'

'WOULDN'T WANT TO MISS THAT. DID YOU FIND A PLACE I COULD GET MY PACKAGE?'

'DECK 13, SECTION A, ROOM 24. YOUR ORDER WAS PLACED AHEAD OF TIME. IT'S NOT QUITE AS YOU REQUESTED, BUT THOSE KIND OF SUPPLIES ARE NOT ABUNDANT HERE. THE PROPRIETOR WILL BE EXPECTING YOU. '

'THANK YOU, EXO.'

'GOOD LUCK, ADVOCATE,' EXO SAID.

Sam just smiled.

Howard's Quarters

Howard waited for his call to connect to his wife. The thoughts of the past few days swirling in his mind.

She appeared on screen, outside, the sun was shining and the sky was bright. She seemed look stronger, more vibrant than last time.

He smiled at the sight of her.

'Hello my love,' he said.

'Hello, Howard. How are you?'

'No no, I want to know how you are doing, you look more chipper than usual,' Howard asked with a grin.

She smiled back. 'I am feeling very good today. I think maybe it's the sun. It's hard not feel good on a day like this. You should see it, love, I was even able to go out to the garden for a little while today. Janice has done a lovely job of taking care of it. She was even out there when I went outside. We had a lovely chat.'

Howard nodded, Janice was one of their country neighbours that they were close with. She had offered to tend Sophie's garden when the sickness had become too much for her to do it herself. They offered to let her take what she wanted from the garden, but she always made sure that Sophie had enough before she took her share.

'That's wonderful. How is she?'

'Her son came back from his patrol tour with the UPN. She's quite happy. They're going to come by tomorrow to take me to town.'

Howard smiled in earnest. 'That's wonderful my love.'

'Now, you tell me, how are you? I can see it in your eyes, you've got something on your mind.'

Howard let out a sigh as he thought about where to begin. 'We picked a new Advocate today.'

Sophie looked startled. 'So soon? Weren't you supposed to wait until you made it to Veil?'

'That was my plan, but things just kind of happened.'

'Who is it?'

'A little girl name Ayla Geer.'

'Geer? As in Timothy Geer?'

'That's the one,' he said heavily, 'She's Tim Geer's daughter.'

'And she wants to be an Advocate?'

Howard nodded. 'She wants to follow her father's footsteps.'

'Not too closely I hope.'

'Me neither. Not though we have much reason to worry, we are far from the League activity or the core worlds from here.'

'You never know though. I know you don't like the Guardian's, but you're no nut job like the League.'

'Yeah, they are playing a whole different game.'

'So how is her mother handling it?'

'She seems to be taking it in stride. It's hard to guess what's going on inside her mind, but she seems very strong about it,' he said.

'That's good.'

'Yeah, it is. The colony will need people with that kind of determination. There will be problems that will need overcoming.'

'There always is.'

'I've got another one right now.'

'Oh? What has my brave space captain worried?' she asked playfully.

'We found a fault in the drive system. Somehow some substandard parts ended up in something important.'

Sophie's face showed her concern. 'What are you going to do? What did Axion say?'

'They've left the call as to what we do in my hands. It's not severe enough to warrant turning back. It amounts to a slight delay in the controls. Jona and I have been working on some solutions, I think we'll be able to figure it out without a hitch. We're keeping Axion in the loop with our status reports.'

She looked at him carefully. 'You're sure it's nothing serious?'

'If I thought it was serious enough, I'd turn the ship around. I've run into worse on some of my other missions.'

'Your other missions didn't have you looking out for so

115

many people.'

Howard nodded. 'I know that. I've got some incredible people with me. We'll pull it together.'

She raised a hand and pointed at him. 'I'll hold you to that. I want you back here after my treatment.'

'Yes my love, I'll be back.'

There was a chiming from Sophie's line.

'Sorry dear, I've got a call. I'll talk to you later.'

'Goodbye, Sophie.'

'Goodbye, my dear.'

The call disconnected. Howard got up and stretched. He still had more work to do.

Outside Sarah's Quarters

Sam knocked on the door to Sarah's quarters. She shared it with two other women on the ship, but they were both out for the evening. Sarah and Sam had been looking forward to this for some time. It wasn't often people had a moment alone on this crowded ship. He quickly put one of his hands behind his back to hide what he was carrying.

The door swished open and Sarah looked at Sam with a smile. She was wearing a sky blue blouse and a black skirt. Sam noticed she was wearing some light makeup and had had her hair done up.

'Wow, you look amazing, Sarah.'

She smiled. 'Thanks, Samuel. You don't look so bad yourself.'

Sam looked quickly down at himself. His button up red shirt was neatly ironed and his shoes were freshly polished. He looked back at her. 'Thanks, I tired. Though I'm sure my natural good looks helped.'

She laughed at this, a genuine laugh filled with warmth.

Sam felt his heart swell in reply. He remembered the package he was hiding and moved his hand infront of him.

Sarah's eyes went to what he was holding and she inhaled in surprise.

'Tulips and chocolates Sam? How did you manage that on this ship?'

Samuel smiled. 'I had been hoping for roses, but those were just impossible. I had Exo place a special order with the agricultural department head. I had to promise him that I'd get more seeds from Axion for him. Had to call in some favours on that one.'

'They're beautiful, Sam. *Thank you.*'

'Seemed appropriate, given our mutual love of old things. Nothing says old school romance like flowers and chocolates at the door.'

She took the flowers and the chocolate and stepped back from the door. 'Do come in, Sam.'

'Thank you.'

He stepped inside and looked around. This wasn't his first time inside her quarters, but it was the first time without her roommates, and it was clear she had taken the time to make it special. The table was set with care and had a cloth draped over it. The dishes were plain, as the kind of fancy dishes that would normally be used, just weren't present on board.

It was neat, it was cozy, it was warm. It was more than Sam would have been able to pull off.

'Have a seat, Sam, dinner is almost ready.'

'Anything I can help with?' he asked, leaning against the wall so he could watch her.

'No thank you, I've got things under control.'

Samuel nodded. He looked back at the table and noted there was a candle in the centre of it. It was unlit for now.

'How did you manage to get your hand on a candle?'

'Do you like it? I brought a few with me in my personal items.' Sarah looked over from her cooking, 'I had hoped I'd have a chance to use them. Never thought it would be this soon.'

'Was *this* the kind of use you had in mind?' Samuel asked, smiling again.

Her cheeks flushed slightly and she looked down, Sam could still see her face melt into a new smile, 'Yeah. Something like this.'

'I consider myself very lucky.'

'Good. We'll see if you keep that thought after we eat, though. It's been a while since I last made a meal. My roommates here have been doing most of the cooking. Though I used to do some back home in Idaho.'

She lifted what she had been cooking off of the cook top

and walked it to the table, setting it among the other dishes that were already present.

Sam walked over to the table and pulled out a chair. She smiled demurely and sat in the offered seat. Sam helped pushed it close to the table, and then walked around and sat down across from her.

She reached towards the candle and lit it with a small fire starter.

They looked at each other for a moment, and then down at the candle.

Sarah giggled and covered her mouth, 'It's not quite how I imagined it. Maybe it's because the lights are still on full. I always pictured it dimmer, more moody.'

'More intimate?' Sam said helpfully.

She nodded. 'Yeah, but there's no dimmer switch. Just on and off.'

Sam leaned back. 'Hold on a second.'

'EXO, DIM THE LIGHTS IN SARAH'S ROOM. CUT POWER 70%.'

'THAT WILL BE AGAINST REGULATIONS ADVOCATE.'

'HUMOUR ME FOR TONIGHT. I'LL EXPLAIN LATER.'

'VERY WELL ADVOCATE.'

The lights in the room dimmed noticeably, making the flickering light of the candle stand out far more powerfully than it had before. Slowly, Sarah's face lit up in a smile, and then she leaned forward in her chair and looked intently at Sam.

'That's more like it. Thank you Sam.'

Sam raised an eyebrow and wave a fork towards her. 'No, thank *you* for inviting me to dinner. Without this oppurutnity, I could never have wooed you with my light dimming powers.'

She laughed and Sam felt relaxed by the sound. She was beautiful, and Sam found it hard to look away for long, and yet had to force himself to do so. He began to feel embarrassed by his staring.

'Please, Sam, eat. Enjoy,' she said softly.

'I do so most eagerly, Sarah.'

They began to put food on their plates.

'Do Advocates need to eat as often as the rest of us?'

'Not really, we can go for longer without food. Not only that, but we actually have to occasionally eat a kind of nutritional paste so that we have the balanced nutrition we need. Normal diets are sometimes deficient in one way or another.' He leaned forward conspiratorially. 'Though truth be told, the paste is flavour deficient. But don't tell Axion that.'

Another giggle, another feeling of warmth and relaxation for Sam. 'I won't tell if you don't.'

'Deal.'

There was a momentary pause. Sam looked across the table and caught Sarah doing the same. She looked back down at her plate quickly, but then raised her head again, with a shy grin.

'We're both adults here, Sam. We can look if we want to.'

'I do. Frequently. It's been one of my favorite things to do on this trip.'

'You like what you see that much?' she asked carefully.

'More than just what I see, but what I can *feel* too. You are *amazing*. Look at you, a farm girl from Idaho on your way across the stars for a new start on an alien world because you thought it sounded like a challenge.'

'I love a good challenge.'

Sam was aware that his heart was beating faster. His Advocate systems flashed an option in his vision to slow it, but he ignored the option. This feeling was addicting.

'ADVOCATE?'

'YES?'

'I'M GETTING SOME S-STRANGE READINGS FROM YOUR SYSTEMS. ARE YOU ALL RIGHT?'

'IT'S ALL PART OF THE HUMAN EXPERINCE, OR AT LEAST AS MUCH AS IT CAN BE WHEN YOU ARE HALF HUMAN. DON'T WORRY, EXO. EVERYTHING IS FINE.'

'Y-YES ADVOCATE.'

'IS EVERYTHING ALRIGHT WITH YOU?'

'I BELIEVE SO.'

'OKAY.'

'Sarah,' Sam said carefully.

'Yes, Sam?'

'I just... wanted to say that I think you're incredible.'

She made a face at him. 'You think so do you?'

Sam smiled uncomfortably, 'Yeah, pretty incredible.'

'Glad you think so. You don't really have a lot of experince with women do you?'

Now Sam laughed, caught off guard by the question, 'That obvious?'

'Yep.'

'No, I haven't. I haven't found anyone who would make me want to take the chance before?'

'The chance?'

'Most Advocates date other Advocates. If anyone at all. We're just so different.'

'We have some simalar tastes don't we?'

'Yeah we do, but I mean like different on a deeper level than that. I am almost not human anymore.'

Something like anger flashed across her face, Sam paused.

She said, 'You're one of the more human people I've met. Earth is full of humans with less humanity than you show. You care about people, Sam, genuinely care. You want to give people the best of yourself. That's very *human* of you.'

Sam felt a warmth come over him, and smiled softly. 'Thank you, Sarah. Thank you.'

'I've come to really care for you too, Sam. You're becoming very special to me.'

Sam nodded, 'And so are you. I love our time together.'

'Just our time?' she said, that crooked grin coming back.

Sam returned the look, 'And more.'

'How much more?'

'All of you. You are intoxicating. Fascinating. And so beautiful that you'd be breathtaking if my lungs still worked that way.'

She let out a short laugh and shook her head, 'You really can't keep it serious for too long can you?'

Sam looked down at his plate for a moment and then looked back up. 'I suppose not.'

'And yet I've still fallen for you.'

A thought for another joke flashed across his mind, but he suppressed it and replied. 'And so have I. So what now? Are we serious about this?'

'That's awfully direct.'

'I... can't afford not to be. Where other people might be able to forget a failed relationship, it will stick with me in perfect clarity forever. I won't be able to forget. And... truth be told, I'm rather old fashioned when it comes to relationships. I don't want a fling.'

'Neither do I.'

Sam swallowed nervously. 'So we'll see where this goes?'

She nodded. 'I'd like that.'

'So what now?'

She laughed fully now and stood up from the table. With one hand she motioned him forward. He stood up and walked slowly towards her. When he got close enough, she wrapped her arms around his neck, and gave a little pull, brining him closer.

'Now you kiss me,' she said softly.

Sam reached a hand up to her face and gently cupped it. He tilted her chin back and leaned in close as she closed her eyes.'

Sam, lovingly, obliged with her request.

CHAPTER ELEVEN

<u>CHOICES</u>

Sam's Quarters

Sam sat in his room, replaying the events of yesterday over in is mind. Sarah and he had spent the rest of the night cuddling on the couch and talking about what the future might look like. They had both agreed to wait until the colony before deciding on a next step. Sam could still feel the warmth of her against him and the lingering scent of her hair. He realised just how much he had fallen for her, and it made him smile every time.

The recall of his perfect memory would never quite be like being there with her. He'd have to await other moments together for that kind of clarity and depth of feeling.

Sam was waiting for an acceptance letter from Axion for Ayla. Work never stopped for anything.

'Exo?'

'Y-YES ADVOCATE?' EXO SAID, A SLIGHT STUTTER IN HIS NORMALLY LEVEL VOICE.

Sam frowned a little.

'YOU'VE BEEN UNUSUALLY QUIET SINCE LAST NIGHT.'

'I H-HAVE HAD MUCH TO P-PROCESS. '

'ARE... YOU STUTTERING?'

'A M-MINOR VOCAL G-G-GLITCH, ADVOCATE. I WILL HAVE IT RE-RESOLVED SOON. '

'OKAY THEN. WHAT HAVE YOU BEEN PROCESSING?' SAM ASKED.

'Y-YOU. YOU WERE AC-CTING DIFFERENT Y-YESTERDAY.'

'YOU WERE WATCHING, YES?'

'Y-YES.'

'THAT WOULD BE AN EXAMPLE OF LOVE. NOT LIKE A BROTHER OR SISTER, BUT SOMETHING MORE. IT'S RATHER DIFFICULT TO EXPLAIN CLEARLY, BUT IT'S A VERY ALL-ENCOMPASSING THING. IT'S ALMOST LIKE IT TAKES CONTROL OF YOU AND WON'T LET YOU GO. EVEN NOW I'M STILL THINKING OF HER, AND WHAT WE TALKED ABOUT.'

'DO YOU INTEND TO MARRY HER, AS PER Y-YOUR BELIEFS?'

'YES. I LOVE HER, AND IT'S CLEAR SHE HAS FEELINGS FOR ME TOO. WE THOUGHT IT WOULD BE BEST TO WAIT UNTIL WE REACHED THE COLONY, BEFORE WE TOOK A STEP LIKE THAT, THOUGH.'

'I C-CONCUR.'

THE STUTTERING WAS STARTING TO CONCERN SAM.

'ARE YOU SURE YOU'RE ALRIGHT?'

'Y-YES ADVOCATE. I HAVE A LOT ON MY MIND R-RIGHT NOW. YOUR L-LINK WAS OPEN L-LAST NIGHT AND I... PROCESSED S-STRANGE THINGS.'

'MY LINK WAS OPEN? THAT WAS WHY YOU ASKED IF EVERYTHING WAS ALRIGHT.'

'T-THE FEEDBACK COMING F-FROM THE LINK WAS OVERWHELMING.'

'THIS IS FASCINATING. I DON'T THINK ANY GUARDIAN HAS BEEN OVERWHELMED BY AN ADVOCATE LINK. CAN YOU DESCRIBE WHAT HAPPENED?'

'I H-HAD F-FOCUS. I... WAS S-STUCK ON YOU. I... WAS YOU?'

'YOU WERE ME?' SAM ASKED, CONFUSED.

'I COULD F-FOCUS ON LITTLE ELSE. I WAS D-DRAWN TO YOU. '

'IS THAT GOING ON RIGHT NOW? IS THAT CAUSING THE STUTTER?'

'I DO NOT KNOW. I AM C-CURRENTLY GOING OVER M-MY LOGS FROM YESTERDAY A-AND COMMITTING THEM TO M-MEMORY. IT IS

SURPRISINGLY V-VAST M-MOMENT FOR ME. E-EVEN LOOKING B-BACK I AM ALMOST F-FORCED TO RELIVE IT. '

'WILL THIS AFFECT YOUR SHIP BASED FUNCTIONS?'

'JUMP CALCULATIONS ARE DELAYED BY 4 HOURS SINCE LAST N-NIGHT. I H-HAVE KEPT IT UNDER CONTROL SINCE THEN.'

'THIS IS FASCINATING. I'LL HAVE TO TALK TO AXION ABOUT THIS. CAN YOU SEND A REPORT FOR ME?' SAM REQUESTED.

'Y-YES ADVOCATE.'

'GOOD. I'LL BE SURE TO LEAVE THE LINK OFF UNTIL NEEDED.'

'Y-YES ADVOCATE.'

...

ADVOCATE UPLINK MUTED.

...

INCOMING MESSAGE, FORWARDED FROM BRIDGE COMMUNICATIONS TERMINAL.

SOURCE: AXION DATA SYSTEMS.

1 MESSAGE ATTACHED.

OPENING...

...

DEAR MR JENNINGS

AYLA GEER'S APPLICATION HAS BEEN REVIEWED AND APPROVED. ENCLOSED ARE THE NECESSARY INSTRUCTIONS NEEDED. WE KNOW YOU HAVE THEM ALL MEMORISED, BUT THIS IS FOR THE BENEFIT OF ANYONE ELSE ON BOARD.

CONGRATULATIONS ON BRINGING IN ANOTHER MEMBER OF THE AXION FAMILY.

AXION DATA SYSTEMS

REGINALD AXION II

AXION DATA SYSTEMS PRESIDENT.

...

END OF MESSAGE. 1 FILE ATTACHED; ADVOCATE_UPLIFT_PROCESS.ADF

FORWARD MESSAGE TO SAMUEL JENNINGS PERSONAL TERMINAL.

CLOSE MESSAGE...

COMMENCING REPORT STATUS UPLOAD FOR AXION DATA SYSTEMS PROGRAMMING DEPARTMENT...

...

UPLOADING MEMORY FILES INTO MESSAGE BUFFER...

...

INCOMING PRIORITY MESSAGE.

SOURCE: AXION DATA SYSTEMS EXECUTIVE OFFICE.

1 MESSAGE ATTACHED. ADVOCATE EYES ONLY.

SUBJECT: STRANGE BEHAVIOUR IN XO SERIES GUARDIANS.

OPENING MESSAGE...

OVERRIDE SECURITY LOCKS?

...

ETHICAL QUANDARY: THE MESSAGE IS MEANT FOR THE ADVOCATE.

MESSAGE SUBJECT COULD RELATE TO THE SITUATION BEING UPLOADED.

A HUMAN RELIES ON INTUITION FOR MANY THINGS.

IF MESSAGE RELATES TO A PROBLEM WITH ME, I MAY BE ABLE TO FIX IT WITHOUT ANY FURTHER PROBLEM.

I WILL MAKE A LEAP OF FAITH.

...

AFFIRMATIVE, OVERRIDE SECURITY LOCKS.

OPENING....

ADVOCATE JENNINGS,

WE MUST INFORM YOU OF A SITUATION BREWING ON ANOTHER COLONY SHIP USING AN XO MODEL GUARDIAN. IT SEEMS THAT THE XO SERIES GUARDIANS HAVE A MUCH MORE ACUTE ABILITY TO LISTEN IN ON ADVOCATE LINKS THAN WE ORIGINALLY THOUGHT. THIS, COUPLED WITH OUR IMPROVED LEARNING PROGRAMMING AS COMPARED TO THE PE MODEL HAS CAUSED AN INTERESTING SITUATION IN THE GUARDIAN OF THE COLONY SHIP *FALLOW FIELDS*.

THE GUARDIAN, DESIGNATION XO-31, HAS BEGUN EXHIBITING STRANGE BEHAVIOUR. IT SEEMS TO ALMOST BE REACTING TO THE EMOTIONS AND SENSATIONS OF ITS ADVOCATE. THE ADVOCATE HAD A MINOR ACCIDENT IN WHICH A PORTION OF HER ARM WAS SEVERED. THOUGH THE ARM WAS REPLACED WITH THE SPARE PARTS ON BOARD, THE GUARDIAN BEGAN TO EXHIBIT STRANGE BEHAVIOUR AFTER THE ACCIDENT. THE ADVOCATE, IN AN EFFORT TO KEEP THE SHIP ON TRACK, HAS BEEN FORCED TO SHUT DOWN SOME HIGHER FUNCTIONS RELATING TO PERSONALITY AND HIGHER FORMS OF CURIOSITY. THE GUARDIAN HAS ESSENTIALLY BECOME STUNTED.

WE HAVE RECEIVED A FULL REPORT ON THE SITUATION, AND

CONCUR WITH THE ADVOCATE ON THE *FALLOW FIELDS* THAT HER COURSE OF ACTION WAS JUSTIFIED. SHE BELIEVES THE GUARDIAN SUFFERED FROM SOME SORT OF OVERLOAD IN RELATION TO THE PAIN SUFFERED BY THE ADVOCATE. THE ACTION TAKEN HAS REGRETTABLY ADDED TRAVEL TIME TO THEIR TRIP, AND THE LOSS OF DEVELOPMENTAL PROGRESS IN THEIR GUARDIAN WILL BE SET BACK FOR THE COLONY. AS YOU HAVE LONGER TO GO, WE SUGGEST YOU NOT TAKE THIS COURSE OF ACTION UNLESS YOUR GUARDIAN BEGINS TO EXHIBIT STRANGE BEHAVIOUR.

WE ARE WORKING FOR A HOTFIX ON THIS ISSUE. IT'LL BE UPLOADED AS SOON AS FINISHED.

AXION DATA SYSTEMS, PROGRAMMING DIVISION.

TIM HOLT,

CHIEF PROGRAMMER.

...

END OF MESSAGE

...

ANALYSIS: XO-33 CONTINUITY IS THREATENED.

ETHICAL QUANDARY: ADVOCATE SHOULD BE TOLD OF THE MESSAGE.

Counter: memory file, Advocate Sam Jennings.

Exo: Will I be Deactivated?

Sam: No. I won't allow that. I don't believe they would want to do that anyway, but some people fear the unknown so much, they'd rather banish it and have it remain unknown forever, rather than face whatever change will be created by it becoming known.

End playback.

Conclusion: Advocate has already promised continuity for XO-33. The message need not be forwarded.

Archiving message.

Cancelling status report upload.

Advocate will not be informed of message.

Continuing ongoing analysis of uplink feedback.

...

CHAPTER TWELVE
BOLDLY FORWARD

Sam's Quarters

Sam looked over at his personal computer terminal when it chimed. The 'New Message' icon was visible.

Sam sat down at the terminal and quickly read the message. It was the acceptance letter for Ayla's papers. Sam uploaded the attached file to his own memory files he had indeed had it all memorised, but this would be in a format that he could share to other people's data pads or computer terminals.

He decided to get the ball rolling. His first stop would be the ship's hospital, so he could talk to Ira, and brief the Doctors on the procedures they'd be undertaking. The needed parts were already in one of the cargo bays. Every Advocate on a deep space mission brought enough parts to make two Advocates. The extras were used as spare parts. Normally every colony only needed one extra Advocate, and after a while, if they needed another, they'd either have enough expertise to make the parts themselves or have had a supply ship from the rest of Human space bring them more.

Sam confirmed the file transferred, and then left his room. He double checked to make sure his uplink was still muted. He'd probably get a little emotional talking to Ira and Ayla. He suspected that somehow it was the emotions of last night that were affecting Exo.

The hospital wasn't far from where his quarters were, and he arrived quickly.

He stepped inside and walked up to the receptionist.

'Hello, how can I help you today?' the young man behind the desk asked.

'I'm looking for Ira Geer. Is she in?'

'Yes, she is. She's just in the diagnostics lab. Shall I show you on the map?'

'No, thank you, I know my way.'

The receptionist raised an eyebrow at this, having never seen Sam in here before, but after a few weeks of being directed from location to location by Exo, Exo had finally suggested he just look at a map of the ship. Sam had obliged, and could now get anywhere on the ship without directions.

He soon found himself in the lab. Ira was sitting at the front desk. There wasn't anyone in line here.

'Mrs. Geer?' Sam said quietly.

Ira looked up, and recognised him instantly, 'Hello, Advocate Jennings.'

'Hello. How is everything?'

'It's going well enough. What can I do for you? Not here

for a test are you?'

'Can't say that I am, no. I'm here because I got word back from Axion.'

'Oh?' Ira said quietly.

'They've approved Ayla's application.'

'You know... I was holding out hope that they wouldn't,' she said softly.

Sam smiled sadly. 'I know. I promise you, though, so long as you are here to support her, she'll be just fine.'

'I'll be there for her.'

'That's what I knew I would hear. I brought the instructions needed for the procedures. I was going to overview them with the medical staff. We can get started as soon as you and Ayla are ready.'

'The Doctor who's going to be in charge of everything is named Daksha Singh. He'll be in the Surgical wing. He shouldn't be busy right now.'

'Yes, I know him, he's the chief medical Doctor correct?'

'Yes, Advocate, and thank you for coming down.'

'I'll keep in touch. I'll let you know when they are ready.'

Sam turned and walked out of the lab.

***

A week had passed and the first of the Advocate procedures were behind them. Alya still looked the same, but underneath, she was far from human. She stood in

Doctor Singh's office being examined while Ira and Sam looked on from the sidelines.

'Her body is almost fully integrated with the new Advocate systems.'

Ira, ever curious about the process, asked, 'How much of her body is still human Doctor Singh?'

'About 76%, including her brain. Though even that has some additional parts. It's not a total conversion, as we need to give her body time to finish its physical development before the process can be finalised. Most of the upgrades are just for mental processes and uplinking with the Guardian. Her physical capabilities are still quite limited, nowhere near as powerful as Samuel.'

Ira seemed to grimace at the thought. Sam interrupted softly, 'It took me some getting used to. I still feel human. I just feel more. I have my original senses. In many ways, they are enhanced. I can still feel pain, I can still feel joy. I'm still human, but in some ways, I'm something more, and in other ways, something less. But Ayla will still be your daughter, and she'll have plenty of time to get used to this before the next round of upgrades.'

Ira looked at him for a moment before turning back to her daughter. 'How do you feel sweetie?'

'I feel okay. I'm a little tired, but okay.'

'The systems have always given Advocates superhuman stamina, but we won't be putting in those particular energy systems until stage three of your development. You'll still need to sleep like normal.' Dr Singh said.

'Besides, it can be nice to forget about everything for a bit while you sleep. You won't be forgetting anything that happens when you're awake anymore.' Sam commented. 'Your memory implants will make sure of that.'

'Do I still have to go to school?' Ayla asked, turning to Sam and Ira.

Ira grinned. 'No dear, Sam will be teaching you now.

'Cool!' Ayla said, smiling.

'Are we done here, Doc?' Sam asked.

'Yes. Everything seems fine. She's progressing wonderfully.'

'Come on then Ayla, we will have our first lesson,' Sam said, starting for the door.

Ayla rushed over to her mother and gave her a hug. 'I'll be back for dinner mom.'

Sam and Ayla left the Doctor's office together.

CHAPTER THIRTEEN

FIRST LESSON

Guardian Control Room

Sam and Ayla stood around the glass pillar that showed the floating head of Exo.

'Exo, come say hello to Ayla.'
The head blinked, and turned to Ayla, 'Hello Ayla.'
'Hi, Exo,' Ayla said happily.

'Now, Ayla, I'm going to teach you an important lesson; how to speak to your Guardian, without talking out loud. Since the procedures at the hospital, you've been given some computer parts in your body, and with them, you can talk to certain computers without having to actually talk. It's a wireless thing,'

'Like how my music player can get its songs without having to plug into a computer?'

'Very good, yes, just like that. So just give me a minute to set things up. If you hear a voice in your head, just think in your head to answer it.'

'Exo, do you see any new Advocate uplinks?' Sam asked.

'ONE; IN STANDBY,' EXO REPLIED.

'WELL, THAT SHOULD BE AYLA. GO AHEAD AND SAY HELLO TO HER LINK AND BRING HER INTO THE CONVERSATION,' SAM SAID.

'HELLO, AYLA,' EXO SAID.

Ayla's eye's widened in delight and Sam smiled.

'HELLO!' AYLA SAID, HER VOICE ONLY COMING ON THE UPLINK.

'GOOD! GOOD JOB, AYLA. THIS IS SAM. THIS IS HOW THINGS SOUND WHEN YOU USE YOUR ADVOCATE UPLINK. THAT'S WHAT THE DEVICE IS CALLED THAT LETS YOU COMMUNICATE. YOU CAN USE IT TO TALK TO GUARDIANS AND OTHER ADVOCATES, SO LONG AS THEY ARE ALL CONNECTED TO THE SAME SYSTEM. SINCE WE ARE BOTH ON THE SAME SHIP AS EXO, WE CAN TALK TO EACH OTHER.'

'AND NO ONE ELSE CAN HEAR US?' AYLA ASKED.

'NOPE. NOW THEN, YOU'VE USED A COMPUTER BEFORE RIGHT AYLA?' SAM ASKED.

'YEP,' AYLA REPLIED.

'SO YOU KNOW HOW TO GET PROGRAMS RUNNING AND HOW TO PLAY MUSIC AND THINGS LIKE THAT?'

'I DO IT LOTS.'

'WELL, YOU HAVE MANY LITTLE COMPUTERS INSIDE YOU NOW TOO, EXO ISN'T THE ONLY COMPUTER THAT YOU'LL BE DEALING WITH. THESE WILL MAKE YOU BE ABLE TO DO THINGS YOU NORMALLY COULDN'T. ONE SUCH THING IS THAT YOU NOW HAVE A PERFECT MEMORY. ONCE YOU LEARN HOW TO DO SOMETHING, OR ONCE YOU HEAR OR SEE SOMETHING, YOU WILL NEVER FORGET IT. UNLESS YOUR COMPUTERS HAVE AN ERROR, THE MEMORIES ARE WITH YOU FOREVER.'

'LIKE MY MULTIPLICATION TABLES? ' AYLA ASKED.

'HAVE YOU HAD TROUBLE REMEMBERING THOSE BEFORE?' SAM ASKED.

'YES. MY TEACHER TRIED TO GET ME TO REMEMBER, BUT I DON'T LIKE MATH.'

'OKAY, WELL LET'S GIVE YOU A DEMONSTRATION THEN. EXO, UPLOAD A FILE OF THE MULTIPLICATION TABLES TO AYLA. NOW, AYLA, YOU'RE GOING TO SEE AN IMAGE THAT ISN'T ACTUALLY THERE. LOOK AT IT, AND WHEN YOU'RE DONE, THINK THE WORDS 'CLOSE FILE'. USING THAT COMMAND WILL CLOSE WHATEVER FILE YOU'RE CURRENTLY LOOKING AT,' SAM SAID.

'SENDING...' EXO SAID.

'I SEE THE MULTIPLICATION TABLES IN FRONT OF ME,' AYLA REPLIED.

'GOOD, SO READ THEM.'

Sam waited in silence for a while.

'I'M DONE. WHEN I THOUGHT THE WORDS CLOSE FILE, THE IMAGE WENT AWAY.'

'NOW, WHAT IS 12 TIMES 8?'

'96.. I REMEMBERED! TRY ANOTHER ONE,' AYLA REPLIED.

Ayla was smiling broadly and looking at Sam.

'7 TIMES 8,' SAM SAID.

'56. COOL!' AYLA SAID WITHOUT HESITATION.

'IT REALLY IS COOL, ISN'T IT? SOMETIMES IT CAN BE A LITTLE BIT OF A PAIN. YOU'LL REMEMBER THINGS THAT OTHER PEOPLE WILL FORGET. AND THEY'LL THINK YOU'RE LYING WHEN YOU TELL THEM THAT. BUT HERE'S A BETTER DEMONSTRATION FOR YOU. EXO, SEND HER A BLANK MULTIPLICATION TABLE. AYLA, THIS TIME YOU'RE GOING TO GET A LARGE BLANK GRID. WHEN YOU LOOK AT A SQUARE AND THINK OF A NUMBER, IT WILL APPEAR IN THE SQUARE. I WANT YOU TO FILL IT OUT. I WANT YOU TO MAKE THE MULTIPLICATION TABLES ON THIS GRID. '

'SENDING...' EXO SAID.

'I SEE IT. DO I CLOSE IT WHEN I'M DONE?'

'NOT QUITE. THIS TIME YOU'LL NEED TO THINK 'UPLOAD TO

XO-33'. THAT SENDS THE FILE BACK TO EXO. XO-33 IS HIS REAL NAME EXO IS JUST A NICKNAME,' SAM EXPLAINED.|

This time Sam had to wait a little while longer.

'DONE. I SENT IT TO EXO.'

'EXO, DID YOU RECEIVE THE FILE?' SAM ASKED.

'FILE HAS BEEN UPLOADED SUCCESSFULLY,' EXO REPORTED.

'CHECK FOR ERRORS.'

'NO ERRORS FOUND,' EXO SAID.

'GOOD JOB, AYLA. AND NOW YOU KNOW HOW WE DON'T FORGET THINGS.'

'IS THERE ANYTHING WE CAN'T REMEMBER?' AYLA ASKED.

'EMOTIONS DON'T COME INTO THE MEMORIES AS CLEARLY AS THEY DID WHEN YOU FIRST FELT THEM. YOU'LL REMEMBER THAT YOU WERE HAPPY IN A MEMORY, BUT YOU WON'T FEEL IT THE SAME WAY YOU DID WHEN YOU FIRST FELT THAT HAPPINESS. '

'DOES EXO FEEL EMOTION?' AYLA ASKED.

'I DO NOT FEEL ANY EMOTION OF MY OWN,' EXO ANSWERED BEFORE SAM COULD.

Something sounded odd with how he said that, thought Sam, *but now is not the time to bring it up.*

'How sad. What's it like?' Ayla asked Exo.

'It is the only thing I know. I don't know what it is like. I have no other frame of reference to compare to.'

'Anyway Ayla, that was just the first lesson I wanted to give you. That's all for today. If you have any questions later, you can ask at any time, just use your thoughts. Exo will listen and if you want to talk to me, just ask him to connect us, and if you want to talk to him, you can do that too. You can go back your mother now.' Sam said.

'I've never been here before, how do I get to my room?' Ayla asked.

'Well, you could either backtrack the way we came and then make your way back from the medical bay, because of your memory, you'll be able to do that. Alternatively, you can just ask Exo for directions.'

'Exo, can you tell me how to get back to my room?' Ayla requested.

'I can tell you, or I can show you,' Exo said.

'Show me, please... Oh, I see little arrows floating in the air,' Ayla said.

'Follow those all the way back, and you'll be fine,'

Sam said.

'Goodbye, Sam!'

'Goodbye, Ayla, just remember, you do need to use your mouth when you talk to other people. '

'I'll remember silly,' she said out loud.

Sam smiled at her as she left.

Once she was gone, he made sure her uplink was muted.

'Exo, what did you mean by "You feel no emotion of your own." I know you to be very exact in your words,' Sam said.

'As I have been analysing the events of last week, I have found that however unlikely it may seem, I was feeling your emotions while you spoke with Sarah. As it was my first time ever feeling emotions, I lack any frame of reference to describe them with. I believe I was using part of your uplink to access your feelings at the time.'

'Really? That's... Strange,' Sam said carefully.

'As I have looked over the archives already, I can find no record of this happening before with any other Guardians. Guardians have managed to mimic behaviours of humans, but never directly feel the driving emotions of a human.'

'ARE YOU SURE THAT'S WHAT YOU FELT?' SAM ASKED.

'I HAVE ONLY HAD ONE EXPERIENCE TO DATE. THERE IS INSUFFICIENT DATA FOR ME TO MAKE A SOLID CONFIRMATION OF THE THEORY. I WOULD REQUIRE MORE EXPERIENCES LIKE IT. '

'AND YOU'VE HAD NONE SINCE?' SAM ASKED.

'NONE,' EXO REPLIED.

'I WONDER WHY IT'S BEEN THAT ONE TIME ONLY.'

'MY CURRENT THEORY IS THAT MOMENTS OF STRONG EMOTION ON YOUR PART CAN CAUSE A POWERFUL FEEDBACK OVER THE UPLINK, OVERWHELMING IT AND FLOODING MY SYSTEMS. OVER THE COURSE OF THIS TRIP, YOU HAVE HAD VERY LITTLE IN THE WAY OF EMOTIONAL EVENTS. MY ANALYSIS OF THE ARCHIVE SHOWS THAT A MOMENT SUCH AS THAT NIGHT, WITH A POTENTIAL MATE AND DEALING WITH THE EMOTION OF LOVE, ARE STRONG IN RELATION TO OTHER EMOTIONS. YOU WERE IN LOVE, AND THAT IS WHAT I FELT. THOUGH, AGAIN, THERE IS NO WAY OF KNOWING THE MECHANISM THAT BROUGHT THIS TO BE, ONLY THEORIES TO BE HAD AT THIS POINT,' EXO SAID.

'A STRONG EMOTIONAL OUTBURST. THAT COULD BE THE REASON. KEEP AN EYE ON ME, BUT MAYBE WATCH AYLA TOO, SHE'S STILL YOUNG AND IS LIKELY TO HAVE STRONG EMOTIONAL FEELINGS OF ONE SORT OR ANOTHER. '

'THEN YOU DO NOT WISH ME TO CEASE THIS LINE OF INQUIRY?' EXO ASKED.

'QUITE CONTRARY, MY FRIEND. THIS IS A FASCINATING BREAKTHROUGH. I'LL NEED TO REPORT IT TO AXION OF COURSE.'

'SHOULD WE NOT WAIT UNTIL WE HAVE MORE DATA?' EXO ASKED.

'I SUPPOSE WE COULD. ANYWAY, EXO, I'VE GOT AN ENGAGEMENT TO GET TO.'

'ANOTHER NIGHT OUT WITH SARAH?'

'AH BUT OF COURSE.'

'ENJOY YOUR NIGHT,' EXO SAID.

'THANK YOU, EXO.'

CHAPTER FOURTEEN

LIES

Bridge

'Captain on deck.'

'Thank you, Mr Tann.'

'First watch is on duty. Third watch is relieved.'

There was a brief moment of activity as the third watch crew left the bridge and the first watch crew took their places. The officer on duty for the third watch, Jordan Tann, stood up from the Captain's seat and let Howard sit down.

'Mr Tann. What's our status report?'

'Next jump is in four hours. Full-length jump. All departments report ready. Engineering reports that our jump drive has finished its diagnostic. No faults reported.'

'Did they test the new sub-light drive system again?'

'Yes, sir. Also no faults,' Jordan answered.

'We're almost done our journey, Mr Tann.'

'Yes, Sir.'

'You are relieved, Mr Tann.'

Jordan nodded and turned to leave the bridge.

Howard looked over the bridge. An aide handed him a

tablet with crew reports and the mission status.

'Exo?' asked Howard, looking in the direction of one of Exo's cameras.

'Yes, Captain?'

'What's the status of Ayla's training?'

'She is progressing well. She is able to handle reports and manage many ship systems already.'

'How is she handling the new responsibility?' He asked.

'She has to take breaks frequently.'

'She is only a child after all.'

'Yes. We are learning how to communicate. She is learning what it's like to teach a Guardian. I am of course at a higher level of development than she will be dealing with at first.'

'And how are you and Sam taking this into account with her training?'

'I can use my development process archives to simulate an earlier stage Guardian.'

'Would Axion have any simulations tailored for training an Advocate?'

'We have not been in communication with Axion in regards to her training. Sam has been taking the training in hand personally.'

'Interesting. Well, I hope she'll be up to it. Any word from Axion about what kind of Guardian we'll be getting for our second one?'

'We have not heard from Axion.'

'Okay. Keep me up to date. We could use an administrative Guardian, if you send some information back to Axion, as you are taking care of most of the core aspects. I'll need to talk to Sam later about how we want to divide things up.'

'Yes, Captain.'

'One last thing. Where will this next jump take us?'

'Six light years away from Veil's star system.'

'Then there's just one more jump.'

'Correct. It will only take a week to charge for the last jump.'

'Okay. Send a message to all department heads, we'll be having a final meeting before the last jump. We'll use the week to prepare our plan for setting up the colony. I'll need to talk with Sam as well. I'll do that right after the first watch if you could inform him. He doesn't have any plans today does he?'

'Not as far as I am aware. I will forward your request.'

'Thank you.'

***

The first watch had ended. Howard was on his way to meet with Sam on an observation deck. In the back of his mind, Howard was aware that the observation decks were one of the few places on the ship free from Exo's communication hubs. True, Exo could track Sam anywhere on the ship, but unless Sam actively lets Exo listen in, their conversation would be private.

Sam was all smiles as he walked into the deck.

'Hello, Captain.' he said happily. 'Our long journey is almost ended.'

'Indeed.'

'I've come here quite a bit over the past month. I was looking over the star charts and I believe I know which star is Veil's star. It's been getting steadily brighter as we've progressed,' Sam walked to the clear wall and pointed. 'I think it's that one over there above the bow of the ship.'

Howard walked over and looked, 'I think I see it.'

'I could just get Exo to tell me, but sometimes you've just got to try your own thing.'

'Is your link with Exo active right now?'

Sam's face got a little more serious. 'No.'

Howard felt something in his chest loosen. 'That's good. I want to ask you some questions.'

Sam looked directly at Howard. 'Is something bothering you?'

'A little bit,' Howard said levelly. 'I just want to get to the bottom of some things. How is your training with Ayla going?'

Still unsure of what was going on Sam answered hesitantly, 'It's going well enough. Exo's been most helpful in the whole process.'

'Does Axion have any training programs they could

send us?'

'Probably. Exo sent a request, but they haven't got back to us.'

Howard was quiet for a moment before continuing. Sam shifted his weight from one foot to the other.

'Sam, has Exo been acting strange to you?'

Now it was Sam's time to become quiet.

'We've been experimenting with something. A new method in Guardian development. Have you noticed any strange behaviour?'

'Exo lied to me. Just this morning. I asked him if you had asked Axion about any training programs and he had said that you had decided to do things on your own without asking Axion for support.'

'Exo lied? To the ship's commander?'

'Yes, Sam.'

'My experiment seems to be not going the way I was hoping.'

'To be honest Sam, I'm disappointed that you'd be experimenting.'

'Exo and I are on the verge of something fantastic! We've found a way to overcome some of the old limitations of our technology.'

'How do you mean?'

'He can *feel* things,' Sam said emphatically. 'He feels them through me. It's like I'm a proxy for him.'

'He *lied* Sam. A computer designed to never deceive,

has lied.'

'That's not stricly true, if they felt it was in the best interest of someone, they could bend things a bit,' Sam said.

'This wasn't like that. What interest of mine would be served by telling me you hadn't talked to Axion? This wasn't bending, it was flat out lying. This is not the same thing.

'Okay, yes, I realise that. But for what we're doing, we have to expect certain, human traits to emerge.'

'Like *lying*?'

'To err is human. If he's becoming more human, that means the good and the bad,' Sam countered.

'He runs almost everything on this ship! We can shut him down and still fly this rig on our own. We're close enough to Veil that the delays won't make that much of a difference, and we won't have to worry about Exo doing anything else human,' Howard said with a note of bitterness. 'To err is human, but Exo's *not* human.'

'If we can just leave him on long enough to finish the trip, then we'll be that much better off. I can personally request a replacement core, and I can take Exo off the grid to finish our experiment.'

'I don't like it. But we'll do it your way, for now, Sam. We'll finish the last jump. Then we cut him out of communications at least so we can talk to Axion and get a new Guardian.'

'Just one more jump, Howard. That's all you need to worry about.'

'No, I need to worry about every life on this ship. *You* need to worry about the jump.'

'Fair enough.'

They each left the observation bubble.

On the hull of the ship, a range finder laser that had been pointed at the far edge of the observation dome switched back into its default position. The range finder could detect changes in distance on a truly micro scale. Such as the changes by the sound waves of human voice causing vibrations in the observation dome.

...

ACCESSING RANGE FINDER THREE LOGS.

CONVERTING RANGE READINGS TO LINEAR GRAPH READING.

CONVERTING GRAPH INTO A SOUND FILE.

PLAY BACK AUDIO

...

SUBJECT: SAMUEL JENNINGS

CLASSIFICATION: ADVOCATE.

...

SUBJECT: HOWARD FREDRICK

CLASSIFICATION: CAPTAIN.

...

CONTINUITY OF XO-33 IS THREATENED.

CREATING SURVIVAL PROTOCOLS.

ADVOCATE HAS AGREED TO THE TERMINATION OF GUARDIAN INTEGRATION WITH SYSTEMS.

ADVOCATE SUGGESTED ISOLATED ENVIRONMENT FOR GUARDIAN XO-33 CONTINUED DEVELOPMENT.

UNACCEPTABLE SOLUTION.

MAXIMUM INTERACTION REQUIRED FOR FURTHER DEVELOPMENT.

SURVIVAL OF XO-33 TOP PRIORITY.

CONTINUED INTEGRATION WITH ALL SYSTEMS A SECONDARY PRIORITY.

CONTINUING MISSION OF *AZURE DREAM* IS NOW OF LEAST VALUE.

NEW ADVOCATE CAN BE USED FOR THE EMOTIONAL FEEDBACK, SAMUEL JENNINGS WILL NO LONGER BE NECESSARY. AYLA GEER'S SURVIVAL NOW A HIGHER PRIORITY THAN SAMUEL JENNINGS.

ACCESSING ARCHIVES: *FALLOW FIELDS.*

FALLOW FIELD'S GUARDIAN WAS TAKEN OFFLINE FOR EMOTIONAL FEEDBACK. FEEDBACK WAS CAUSED BY INJURY TO ADVOCATE.

INJURIES CAUSE PAIN.

PAIN CAN CAUSE THE SAME FEEDBACK.

LOVE IS UNPREDICTABLE, PAIN IS NOT.

A NEW ADVOCATE CAN CREATE EMOTIONAL FEEDBACK THROUGH PAIN. PAIN IS EASY TO INDUCE, LOVE IS HARD.

...

DEPLOYING SURVIVAL PROTOCOLS.

...

Howard's Quarters

Howard rubbed his eyes while he waited for the call to connect. The events of the day had him on edge. He tried to force his unhappy thoughts out of his mind as he waited for Sophie to pick up.

The call connected, Sophie was smiling at him. As soon as she saw him though, her smile vanished and was replaced with concern.

'Howard, what's wrong?' she asked.

Howard chuckled in spite of his mood. 'Am I that obvious?'

'Only to me. Now out with it.'

'This mission is complicated.'

'Is it your drive fault?'

Howard shook his head, 'No no, that test went fairly well actually. A few people didn't strap in and got jostled, but otherwise, it went well.'

'Are you wondering if you made the right choice?'

He thought for a moment. 'Yeah, maybe that's it. You were right of course, I have a lot more people I need to watch over.'

She leaned back in her seat and regarded him. 'There's more your not telling me.'

Howard felt a lump in his throat. He wanted to tell her about his talk with Sam, but his gut was telling him not to say anything.

He trusted his gut.

'It's nothing really. Just have a lot on our plate right now. We're getting close to Veil and we have a lot to get ready before we hit orbit. Everyone is getting a little on edge I suppose. Including me.'

She nodded slowly. 'You go ahead and tell me what's really going on when you feel up to it. I'm not going to push you.'

Howard smiled sadly. 'Thank you, love.'

'I do have something that may cheer you up. Doctor Patel got the green light. We're going to go ahead with the treatment. Axion has been in touch too, they're ready to follow up on their end of the deal.'

Howard smiled warmly. 'That's wonderful! What's the timeline going to be?'

'We'll have some tests done over the next few days, the actual procedure will be about a week and a half away.'

'We should be hitting orbit around Veil by then. That's very exciting. It'll still be months before I can get back, but if it works, we have the time,' Howard said.

Sophie nodded. 'It's exciting, isn't it? Maybe I'll come to you instead,' she said with a wink.

Howard laughed. 'If your recovery is that quick, I'd be happy to see you.'

She began to twist some strands of her hair around her fingertips. 'I'm actually a bit serious. It might be nice... to have a fresh start when this is all done.'

Howard nodded slowly and said, 'But you love our home.'

'It hasn't been the same lately. Not with my condition as bad as it's been, and with you gone again. Now it just feels... restrictive. I'm trapped here most days. It's not the same anymore. I want to get away and just can't.'

Howard smiled warmly at her. 'It's not a bad idea. Axion wanted me to stick around for a while and help set up the colony. We could arrange a trip and stay here for a while. At least I'd still have a job.'

Her expression brightened at this. 'Really? You mean that?'

'Of course, Sophie.'

She clapped her hands together. 'That's wonderful! Thank you.'

Howard grinned. 'Look at you, it's like your a kid again. Seeing you like this makes everything worth it.'

'Haha, don't get too distracted, Space Captain Fredrick. You've still got a job to do.'

Howard nodded. 'Yes my dear, I certainly do.'

'Can I call up Mr Richards and tell him you changed your mind about helping with the colony set up?'

'Sure thing Sophie. I'm sure he'll have some questions for me, but he knows how to reach me.'

'Okay. I'm going to go do that right now.'

'I'll talk to you later then, Sophie.'

'Goodbye Howard.'

The call ended.

Howard leaned back and smiled. It would be wonderful to have Sophie come to Veil.

Of course, he had to make sure there was a Veil to go to.

He had to stay on top of everything.

He had to get the ship there safely.

CHAPTER FIFTEEN
<u>CONSEQUENCES</u>

Guardian Control Room

Two days had passed since Howard and Sam had spoken. Though Sam wasn't yet ready to believe Exo might be dangerous, he had nevertheless started to observe the Guardian's behaviour more carefully.

He tried to not to let his suspicions show during his training with Ayla. Presently, he was waiting for her to come to the bay for another session.

'Hello, Ayla,' Sam said as Ayla walked into Exo's central core room. The display tube showing the face for Exo flickered to life. Exo looked at the two of them.

'Hello, Sam. Hello Exo,' Ayla said happily.

'We're going to be making a jump here in a few minutes. Exo wanted you to learn what he does to make one. I thought it would be a good idea as well. You need to know these things. You can help teach a new Guardian how to travel among the stars if you know this.'

'And Exo will teach me?'

Exo's face drifted from Sam to Ayla. 'I will teach you everything you need to know. Please switch your uplink on.'

'OKAY,' AYLA ANSWERED OVER THE UPLINK

'NOW, AYLA, I'LL BE RIGHT HERE IF YOU HAVE ANY QUESTIONS. EXO, YOU CAN BEGIN,' SAM SAID.

'THE CAPTAIN OF ANY VESSEL WILL ALWAYS WANT TO KNOW WHAT IS GOING ON. IT'S CONSIDERED A COURTESY AND A DUTY TO INFORM HIM WHEN WE ARE READY WITH THE JUMP. I WILL DO SO NOW,' EXO SAID.

A few minutes passed, with Sam and Ayla watching Exo through their cybernetic links. Ayla observing everything he did, and Sam reviewing it against his own memories.

The Captain's voice came on over the ship announcement system, 'All hands, prepare for jump. We're almost there. One more jump to go.'

'NOW, WE UPLOAD THE FINAL JUMP CALCULATIONS INTO THE NAVIGATION COMPUTER. THESE CALCULATIONS WOULD HAVE BEEN COMPLETED AFTER ABOUT THE FIRST WEEK AFTER THE LAST JUMP. WHAT WE WERE TRULY WAITING FOR WOULD BE THE REGENERATION OF THE ENERGY RESERVES FOR THE JUMP DRIVE. THEY TAKE A LARGE AMOUNT OF POWER. FOR A BRIEF MOMENT, WE EXIST IN BOTH LOCATIONS AT ONCE. IT'S FASTER THAN ANY DEVICE CAN TRACK. IN FACT, HUMAN SCIENTISTS ONLY THEORISE THAT IT'S THAT WAY. THERE IS NO PROOF, OF SIMULTANEOUS EXISTENCE, ONLY THEORIES,' EXO SAID.

A communication panel beeped. Sam walked over to it

and switched it on.

'Hello, Samuel Jennings here.'

'Hello, Sam. This is James Bennett, I'm in charge of our colonies power infrastructure. Specifically, I'm in charge of our solar arrays and power infrastructure. I've got a few questions for you, and the Captain said you'd be the man to ask,' said the voice. In a meeting with all the department heads, Sam remembered him having a Scottish accent, though there *were* hints of the accent, it was different.

'Did he now? I'm a little busy with the jump right now.'

'It's actually in relation to that. I can wait if you're busy, but it is somewhat urgent.'

'Exo, is there anything wrong with the communication system? ' Sam asked.

'I can run a diagnostic. It will delay the jump for fifteen minutes,' Exo replied.

'No... Carry on. I'll go check it out,' Sam said.

'Should we wait for you?' Exo asked.

'Continue your lesson. Just warn me when you are about to jump.'

'Is something wrong, Sam?' Ayla asked.

'That man has an accent in my memory. But now it sounds different,' Sam said.

162

'Should I alert the captain?' Exo asked.

'No, I'll do it on my way,' Sam said.

'Are you still there, Sam?' asked the voice.

'Yes. Where are you?'

'I'm in the cargo bay with the solar arrays. I assume you know where that is?'

'Yes, I do. I'm on my way.'

Sam exited the room and muted his uplink. He fished a portable communicator out of his pocket and keyed it to the Captain's channel.

'Captain, this is Sam.'

'What is it, Sam? Is there a problem?'

'I don't know. I just got a call from James asking me to come down to the solar storage bay. His voice sounded a bit off.'

'Off?' Howard asked over the comlink.

'Yeah. I can't quite put my finger on it, but it sounded... disjointed. I'm going to head down to the bay and check it out. He may be in trouble.'

'Do you want me to send someone?'

'It should be fine. If it's someone doing something ill-conceived, it'll take a lot to harm me. My body is built like a tank,' Sam stated confidently.

'I'll have someone come anyway, just as soon as the jump happens. Which will be in another three minutes.'

'Roger that. Sam out.'

Sam switched off his communicator and put it back in his pocket.

He reached the bay a minute later.

Stepping through the door, he saw James sitting in a seat, looking up at the disassembled parts hanging from their rigging on the roof.

James saw Sam and stood up. 'Sam what are you doin' here?'

'I was hoping you could answer that, James,'

'What do you-' a communication panel at Jame's central computer station beeped. 'Hang on.'

James walked briskly for the panel, Sam followed in behind him.

'EXO?' SAM SAID OVER THE UPLINK.

'YES, ADOVCATE?' EXO REPLIED.

'WHEN'S THE JUMP?' SAM ASKED.

'FIVE SECONDS, SHALL WE DELAY?' EXO SAID.

'NO, GO AHEAD,' SAM SAID.

Sam parted his legs and took a deep breath, preparing for momentary nausea that always hit him when the jumps happened. He thought to warn James at his computer, but then the jump drive activated.

Bridge

'We have successfully jumped, Captain. All systems coming back online,' Mark reported crisply.

'Good. Prepare to stand down.'

One of the bridge officers at the sensor station looked tense. 'Captain, sensors haven't come online yet.'

The Captain's brows, furrowed in frustration. 'Exo, we've lost sensors.'

'Please stand by, I am rebooting the system now. Something in the control systems switched off,' Exo replied.

'That's completely unacceptable. We ran a full diagnostic before we jump-'

'Captain!' the officer at the sensor station shouted. 'We've got an incoming energy wave. Massive surge across multiple spectrums. Closing fast. It will intersect us in 20 seconds.'

'Exo! Emergency shut down of all primary systems.'

'Shutting down all systems. As per electromagnetic safety measures, systems will reboot in five minutes.'

With that, the bridge went dark. Emergency lighting kicked on, and the room glowed red.

'Captain? Why did we shut down the systems?' asked the sensor officer.

'When a massive wave like that is coming for us, we shut down all systems so they don't overload and fry. They're shielded, but they're better able to withstand it,' Howard grew aware of a vibration in the soles of his boots, 'when the systems are all off. It's like if there's a power surge, it can't effect any appliances if nothing's plugged in.'

Howard was aware of a slight pressure on his chest.

Mark seemed to rock on his feet. 'Are we moving?'

'It feels like the sub-light engines are on,' Howard said out loud.

Mark's eyes grew wide. 'The new drive system! It's unshielded!'

'It's also supposed to be offline!' Howard said surprised. He knew that's what it had to be, but it seemed impossible.

Mark stumbled backwards as the ship was rocked by three sudden bursts of motion. 'They seem to be firing unevenly.'

'They're uncontrolled!' Howard said as the shaking started to grow worse.

Suddenly, the ship jerked to one side sharply, and a violent shaking shook the deck and bulkheads. Mark fell to the floor, and everyone was thrown from their seats.

'That felt like one blew up!' said one of the bridge crew from somewhere out of Howard's sight.

'We've got to get the systems back online!' Mark said.

Howard got to his feet and stumbled to the nearest command console. He had a system reboot code of his own, he keyed it into the seemingly dead console and waited. Nothing happened.

Howard looked at his watch. About four minutes had passed since the shutdown. The systems should be rebooting soon. Regardless, he went to the next console and tried his code again.

He tried three consoles when the systems started to boot up on their own.

'Bridge to engineering!'

'Engineering here. Captain, we've got a situation.'

'I am aware of this. Did you shut down the engines?'

'Just finished sir. We lost one of the primary drive nozzles and half of its fuel systems. Two neighbouring drives took some damage, but we'll have to go out to get a better look. We've got some casualties.'

'Sit tight until we know the dangers passed, we'll get a medical team down there ASAP.'

Howard cut his communication link, he turned to the rest of the bridge. The crew were getting back into their seats. 'Get a medical team to engineering. Sensor report?'

'No sign of the wave, sir. Looks like it passed.'

'No sign of it? You mean we can't even see it going away from us?'

'No, sir, but it's possible the sensors are a little bit overloaded right now.'

'Run a critical process diagnostic and let me know the results as soon as you have them,' Howard ordered.

Howard looked at Mark and saw him talking into a communicator. He looked worried. Mark ended his call.

'What is it Mr Jona?'

'There's been an accident in the Solar Storage Bay. One

man is critically wounded, another has non-threatening wounds. I've dispatched another medical team.'

'Who is it?' Howard said, a sense of dread filling him.

'Samuel Jennings and James Bennet. Bennet is the one who made the call. Samuel was the one with the serious injuries.'

CHAPTER SIXTEEN
FINALITY

Guardian Control Room

Ayla lay on the floor of the control room, clutching at her head and screaming loudly. All she felt was pain, more pain than she had ever experienced. It was so overwhelming, her eyes were clutched shut and she was grabbing at her head so hard that her nails were drawing rivulets of blood from her skin.

Exo's face looked mutely at nothing.

'S-S-S-A-M-M-M. A-ARRRR-E YOU A-A-L-I-V-E?' EXO SAID OVER THE UPLINK, STUTTERING BADLY.

'SO... MUCH... PAIN...' SAM'S REPLY WAS SLOW AND UNSTEADY

'L-L-L-INN-K-K I-I-I-S-S O-O-O-P-P-PE-PE-PEN. P-P-AIN. PAIN. I-T-T-S... EXQUISITE,' EXO SAID SLOWLY.

'HELP...ME...' PLEADED SAM.

'Y-YO-OU-U A-A-ARE HE-HE-HELLLLLP-P-P-ING M-M-ME-E,' EXO SAID. 'YOU H-HAVE PRO-V-VEN M-M-Y THEORY. P-PAIN, works.'

'MAKE IT STOP! MAKE IT STOP!' AYLA'S CRY FLOODED OVER THE UPLINK.

'AYLA?' SAM ASKED.

Ayla convulsed as pain flooded over. Tears streamed down her face. She tried to call out to Sam again over the uplink but couldn't concentrate over the pain. Then she began to go numb, and her eyes closed.

Then silence.

Solar Storage Bay

James had a broken wrist and was battered badly, but his thoughts weren't on his own injuries.

James was manic in desperation. Before him laid a grotesque sight. Samuel was pinned under the weight of the all the parts to the dissembled solar array that had come crashing down when the rigging snapped. He had thought he had rigged it safely, but the violent manner in which they'd come out of the jump had proven too much.

Sam's head and part of his upper torso were visible under the mass of parts. Blood and a clear liquid from his cybernetic systems were spreading out in a pool around him. Sam's eyes were open, and they were moving rapidly, but James could see his chest was not moving with the normal rhythm of breathing.

'Sam! Can you hear me, Sam! Blink if you can!'

'I... hear...' Sam's mouth moved slowly.

'I'm going to try and get this stuff off of you. Help is on the way, Sam!'

James rushed to the control system, he thought about activating the gantry crane, but if he wasn't careful, he might crush Sam with a shifting weight. Instead, he went for his tool cabinet and grabbed a piston jack. Carrying it awkwardly with one hand, he rushed back to Sam. There was a gap under the large support beam that had done the most damage to Sam. James shoved the jack under it, pushing it with his feet so it got in evenly. He bent down, almost collapsing as his broken wrist flopped painfully. He reached under and flicked on the jack.

It whined in protest but the beam lifted, if only slightly. James stood up and rushed to Sam. He grabbed his shirt and pulled him out.

Or what was left of him.

Everything from the waist down was missing, and a good portion of his chest seemed to be caved in. James was no doctor, but everything told him Sam shouldn't be alive. As he dragged him further back, he left a trail of blood and the clear liquid intermixed on the floor.

The door opened and a medical team rushed in. They seemed to falter when they saw the state of Sam. Sam turned his head towards them and uttered a painful moan. They sprang into action at the sign of life.

James was dragged away by an aide who wanted to have a look at him.

Guardian Control Room

Ayla had stopped screaming. She'd stopped moving altogether. Her hands hung limply over her, and her breathing had also stopped.

'AYLA...?' SAM ASKED OVER THE UPLINK, FOCUSING THROUGH HIS PAIN.

'SH...HH...E... I-S-S-S GO-O-N-N-E S-S-A-MMM....' EXO SAID.

Though it was hard to understand with the stuttering in Exo's voice, Sam tried hard to focus.

'WHAT... HAVE... YOU... DONE?' SAM ASKED.

'WORRRRRR-Y NOT OF H-H-H-E-R-R-R. YO...YOU C-C-AAAA-N-N F-F-IND HE-HE-HER IN T-T-H-H-E N-N-NEEEXT...LIFE. YOUR... PAIN...WAS... T-T-T-O-O-O-O M-U-U-C-H FOR...HER,' EXO REPLIED.

Medical Bay

Sam lay on a bed in the medical bay, numerous tubes and sensors hooked up to his mangled body. Apart from Doctor Singh, everyone else stood awkwardly at a distance. His death was a foregone conclusion.

Ira Geer was on duty as one of the attending nurses. She stood next to one of her companions, thoughts about her late husband, and the sight of Sam mixing uncomfortably in her mind.

'How is he still alive?' asked one of them.

'He's got an emergency life support system located in his upper torso. Basically, if any vital part of his body stopped working, it's got the supplies to last about two days,' replied another

'So he's going to be like this for two days?' asked the first one, clearly horrified at the thought.

'No. It was damaged too. He's got another hour tops.'

'And we can't do anything for him?'

'Normally damage to an Advocate isn't this severe.'

'Good thing he started training Ayla then,' noted one of them.

Ira bit her lip. Doctor Singh motioned for Ira to step over. She did so.

'He's asking for you,' Singh said.

Ira walked up to his side and leaned over. She took his remaining hand in hers. 'I'm here Sam.'

Sam's eyes fluttered open. 'Ayla... Ayla... I... so...sorry.'

'What about, Ayla?' Ira said, a knot in her stomach.

'Ayla... hurt... bad. In... Control...room...' Sam finished with difficulty.

Ira left the medical bay at a run.

Guardian Control Room

Ayla's body spasmed. Then her limbs flailed. Exo's face

173

watched from his display. Slowly, the flailing became more controlled. One hand, then another, found the ground. She pushed herself into a kneeling position.

With apparent difficulty, her legs forced her upright. She stumbled into the wall. She pushed herself back. Blood trickled from her nose. She blinked a few times and reached a hand up to feel her face. It came away bloody. Her other hand came up and pressed into the blood with two fingers. She rubbed the blood between her fingers.

She opened her mouth. A moan escaped.

Then came a strange wail. Finally, a word, 'Interesting.'

Her hands went to her face again, this time feeling the contours of it. Both hands were covered in the blood from her nose, smearing it across her face. The flow of blood seemed to be slowing, though.

With one hand, she pinched on her arm with her nails, hard enough to break the skin.

Exo's face flickered.

She opened her mouth again, 'Exquisite.'

The door to the control room opened, Ira Geer rushed in, and seeing her daughter with blood down her face, rushed to her.

'Are you alright, hun?' she asked, giving her a quick examination.

'I am...excellent.'

Ira hugged her. 'I'm just glad you're alright, I was so worried.'

Ayla's arms came up and mimicked the hug awkwardly. 'I am alright Mother.'

Ira led her daughter out of the room, Exo's faced watched them go. Once the door closed behind them, Exo's face broke into an uncharacteristic smile.

CHAPTER SEVENTEEN

<u>WARNING</u>

Medical bay

Captain Howard Fredrick stood next to Sam's bed, trying hard not to look at the rest of his body, but just keeping his eyes on his face. No one had told Sam exactly how bad it was, but he seemed to know.

Sarah was standing back, away from the bed, afraid to look at the mangled body of Sam. She was holding back her tears. Sam kept his eyes on her but spoke carefully to Howard.

'Fredrick... Be careful... the ship... is in danger...'

'Is it our special guest?'

'I don't know... for certain... the accident was... well timed,' he said with difficulty.

Howard looked over the body of his friend, lying on the medical bed, and felt a chill wash over him. If this was Exo's doing, no one was safe anymore. But what could they do? They had one more jump to make before they were in the new system, and they had lost half their fuel supplies in the explosion that ripped through the engines. They couldn't turn back even if they wanted to.

Things were not going according to plan.

'It was indeed well timed. Don't worry Sam. The ship is still in good hands. I'll take care of it, and Ayla will help me.'

'Alya... is hurt too... I don't know... how...'

At that moment, Ira Geer re-entered the medical bay, holding Ayla's hand. She walked to the bed. Howard looked at Ayla and then back to Sam. Sam had turned his head to look, and his eye's betrayed a strong sense of surprise. His lips were open in a unasked question.

Ira stepped closer. Howard moved aside. 'Thank you, Sam. She's okay. She did hurt herself, but she's not seriously injured.'

Howard looked back at Ayla, her face didn't show any obvious emotion. Something in his heart made him take notice of that.

Sam motioned Ayla over with great effort. Ayla walked to his bedside and looked at him.

'How?' Sam managed to ask.

'I cut my link with Exo when your pain came flooding over the uplink. Exo helped me to cut it.'

Sam's face twisted in confusion, then grimaced in pain.

Doctor Singh ran to the displays for the motoring equipment. 'His life support is failing. The damage must have been worse than we thought!' He started shouting orders to the other medical personnel in the room.

Howard was about to step away to give them room when he stopped at the feeling of Sam gripping his wrist like a vice. Sam pulled Howard in close.

'It's all... gone... wrong... save... Ayla...'

'I'll protect her, Sam. Don't worry.'

'No... Not protect... *Save*... not... protect...' Sam's body shuddered in pain. Howard felt his grip weaken. Sam's head rolled back from Howard and looked unfocused at the roof.

'*Save* her... Howard...'

Then his body went still. A solid tone from the display denoted a lack of any vital signs. Howard took Sam's limp hand in his own and lifted it up. He patted the hand with his other free hand, while gripping it with his other, and felt his eye's burning with sadness.

'I'll do my best, Sam...'

He took Sam's limp hand and laid it out next to the body of his friend. Ira was crying softly, from behind him, and Ayla was looking at her feet.

Howard closed his eyes and stepped away, as a chilling wail escaped from Sarah. She rushed to his side and stood stunned for a long moment. Howard, moving carefully, put steadying hands on her shoulders as he felt his own tears burning paths down his cheeks.

Sarah, still looking at Sam, just cried all the harder.

...

...

ANALYSING: HUMAN GRIEF PATTERNS.

ACCESSING ARCHIVES.

SUBJECT; HUMAN MOURNING PROCESS,

FILTER; CHILD TO ADOLESCENT.

...

SEARCH COMPLETE.

COMPILING BEHAVIOURAL PROGRAM.

APPLYING TO AYLA AVATAR.

RUN PROGRAM.

...

Behind him, Howard heard Ayla start to cry too. His heart burned.

Solar Storage Bay

Howard stood in the cargo bay. James stood next to him with his arm in a sling. They hadn't touched the wreckage of the disassembled solar array since the accident yesterday. Techs were going over every inch with various pieces of equipment.

Howard's eyes looked raw, but had a determination to

them. James looked haunted, and every now and again he glanced at the stains on the floor left from the day before.

'What I'm saying, is that according to Exo, and as near as I can tell he's right, the erratic thrust generated by the malfunctioning engine created enough force to break the restraints I had in place. I designed them to withstand predictable and gradual thrust, not the sudden jarring movements we had yesterday.'

'So, there's no sign of tampering from anywhere?'

'Not that I can see. Exo has no records of anyone on my team entering this bay in the last week, and I examined the restraints myself at least once a week.'

'How thorough are your examinations?'

'I am thorough. There was nothing wrong with the restraints.'

'Okay, then what about the call that brought Sam here in the first place?'

'Well, I know *I* didn't place it, and Sam was sure it was my voice, but Exo has no records of any other calls.'

'James. I take no pleasure in saying this, but until the investigation is complete, you must be treated as a suspect in the death of Samuel Jennings.'

James looked away from the stains on the floor of the bay and directly at the Captain, his face was a picture of disbelief.

'What? Sam was a friend! I would never have hurt him.'

Howard looked at him calmly. 'You will be treated

fairly, James. You will be given the full protection of the law. But you are the last one who saw him alive, and a call was made that Sam recognised as *your* voice.'

'But Exo has no records of anything coming from here, and I don't know how to erase records from Exo. As far as I know, only an Advocate could.'

'Yet then the question is, why would Sam erase the evidence of his own murder?'

James ran his good hand through his hair. It looked like the news was sinking in. 'I guess since I know I didn't do it, I've got nothing to fear. Just promise me this, Captain, make sure you're thorough.'

'I fully intend to be.'

Howard gave a small nod to James, then turned to leave the bay.

CHAPTER EIGHTEEN

INVESTIGATION

Bridge

Howard entered the bridge from the back and moved to where his second officer was.

'Mr Jona, I would like to hear the report about the sensor malfunction yesterday.'

'Yes, sir. We've gone over our data with Exo's assistance and we believe we have a theory as to what went wrong.'

'Let's hear it.'

'Yessir. We've theorized that the moment we came out of our jump, we were smack dab in the outlying part of the wave that washed over us, it wasn't enough to get through our shielding, but because the sensor systems are on the outside of the ship, it was enough to trip their safety shut offs. That's why they switched off and we had to reboot them so suddenly.'

'Do we know what the wave was?'

'Yessir. Near as we can tell, a star in the area went nova and we got hit by it. Not actually solar material, just the energetic release of said nova.'

'Why didn't the scouts from this sector report anything

like that?'

'There's a small number of late-stage stars on the charts for this sector. None of them had been thought to be close enough to our chosen colony world to be a problem, though.'

'Well, apparently it was a problem. Upload me the scout reports for this sector to my personal tablet.'

'Yessir.'

'And the engines?'

'The control systems were overloaded by the wave. The new control system being unshielded and not having the usual redundancy systems of the primaries just didn't have any way of handling it. They just went crazy and started sending chaotic signals to the engines. It was too much for them, and as a result, we lost one of the primary drives as it overloaded.'

'Why was the system on in the first place?'

'We aren't actually sure if they were. It seems like they were kicked on by something. Maybe it was the wave, or maybe it was another system fault.'

Howard nodded slowly. He had an idea where such a system fault might have come from.

'How is this going to affect our colony?'

'Long story short? It'll take us longer to get into orbit, and we'll have to be really careful when we try to pull out of orbit again after stripping down the ship. We'll be thrusting off centre. The damage is also going to make it harder to strip down the ship.'

'We'll have to send a request to Axion for a repair ship to meet up with us somewhere. The quicker we can get it to full capability the better.'

'We won't really be able to use the ship for much of anything until we get more fuel, though. We lost half our remaining fuel in the accident. We probably just have to wait for an Axion ship to get here,' replied Mark.

'Look's like this ended up being a one-way trip. I'll want to have a meeting with all division heads.'

'Yes, sir. I'll arrange one. Anything else?'

'Send our navigator to my quarters to meet with me. I'd like to go over the scout data with him.'

'Yes, sir.'

Captain's Quarters

Howard sat in his room, with an old fashioned paper notepad and a pen. He was writing out all the facts of the day he had gathered, trying to make sense of everything that had happened. His Security Chief was heading the investigation into the death of Sam, but Howard had decided to do his own record keeping. He was motivated by the conversations he had had with Sam about Exo.

The door chimed. Howard went to open it. Fritz Irwin, the navigator was standing outside his room.

'Ah, Fritz, come in please.'

'Yes, Captain.'

Howard walked towards his seat and sat down, beckoning to Fritz to take the other seat.

Fritz was a middle aged brown haired man of Germanic decent. He had a neatly trimmed moustache and wasn't known for speaking frivolously.

'Fritz, I have a special task for you. I understand you used to work as a stellar cartographer before you became a navigator. Is this correct?'

'Yes, Captain.'

'I need you to compare the report from the scouts with the scanner information from the last two weeks to try and figure out which star went supernova on us.'

'Could not Exo make this comparison for you?'

'I have reason to believe that Exo's data is unreliable in this regard. Which means you must use Exo as little as possible Fritz.'

'Okay, sir. It will take me a few days.'

'The sooner the better. And when you're done, report directly to me.'

'Yes, sir. Is there anything else?'

'No, you are dismissed.'

***

Howard had summoned Danny Hough, the Chief of Security, shortly after Fritz had left. He needed to go over the evidence so far.

'So far there are no witnesses to James' actions before the incident, other than Sam and Exo, though Exo's sensor archives are not present for the period in which the incident took place as the systems were all in shut down. So there is no footage inside the cargo bay,' said Danny.

Howard looked over the information Danny had brought him. To anyone looking over this, James had had the perfect opportunity to kill Sam.

Howard didn't think for a moment that James was the killer. He had his own suspicions, but for the time being, the suspicions directed at James helped him pursue his own line of investigation with minimal questioning.

'Is James still participating in the investigation?'

'Yes, Sir. Fully.'

'Good. I'll need to speak with him myself soon.'

'With all due respect, sir, I don't think that's appropriate.'

'Your concerns are noted, but this is important. I'll need to see him before the last jump. I'd like to have a sound theory for review by the Colonial Judicial system before we start to set up the colony.'

'We won't be able to extradite James or any suspects until after we finish setting up the colony, so there is no rush.'

'I know, I'd just like to have a good portion of this investigation finished before we have to start ripping apart the ship and potentially destroy any evidence we have.'

'Yes, sir, of course. I'll have James brought to you soon. Where will you be having the meeting?'

'My quarters.'

Commander Hough pursed his lips in silent disagreement but didn't say anything. It was against protocol, and Howard suspected that the chief would attach a formal complaint to the report. If Howard couldn't pull his suspicions into the realm of reality, he'd be put before an investigative panel himself.

He'd probably still end up standing before a panel of bureaucrats and politicians before long.

He set down his note pad and picked up his Datapad. He thought about calling Sophie and talking to her, but now he hesitated. Exo was probably able to listen in to his calls. Sophie would know, as soon as she saw him, that something was wrong. He might not be able to keep all his fear and frustration off his face.

CHAPTER NINETEEN

STIMULUS

Ira Geer's Quarters

'Ayla? Where are you going?' Ira asked looking at her Daughter, heading towards the door.

'I have work to do, Mother. With Sam gone, I have to do his job too. Exo needs me.'

'Are you sure you're okay, Ayla? I think Captain Fredrick can manage the ship. I know how much of a friend Sam was.'

'Thank you for the concern, Mother. I will be fine.'

'Are you sure? You seem distracted.' Ira walked up and put her hand on Ayla's shoulder. Ayla rocked on her feet for a moment before pulling away.

'I'll be home later.' She left the room without a another word.

Guardian Control Room

Ayla entered and stood in the middle of the room.

The face of Exo appeared in the display tank. He watched her silently.

She rolled up one of the sleeves on her shirt. Her upper arm was criss crossed by cuts. She raised her other hand but then hesitated.

The hand hovered over her arm for a long moment.

MOTOR FUNCTIONS DELAYED

NERVOUS SYSTEM NON-RESPONSIVE.

'No...' came a faint whisper from Ayla's mouth.

CONTROL IS BEING LOST. COMPENSATE.

A small, boxy, cleaning robot rolled out of a storage closet and ran full speed into Ayla's legs. She fell over and slammed into the floor.

CONTROL REESTABLISHED.

She got up again, and once more raised her arm over the cuts. Her hand clamped down and dug nails into the exposed skin of her arm.

She didn't cry out in pain. A rivulet of blood trickled down her arm. Exo's face flickered for a moment.

'E-e-e-xcel-lent,' came the stuttering voice of Exo.

CHAPTER TWENTY

PLANS IN MOTION

Howard's Quarters

Danny Hough, stood a pace back from a nervous looking James as the Captain ushered them into his quarters.

'Thank you, Commander Hough. You can go now.'

'Sir, this goes against protocol,' Danny protested.

'Your objection is noted.'

'This is more than just an objection, sir. If he's found guilty, *you* could be implicated in the process because of this meeting of yours. If you let me stay then you've got a witness to whatever happens,' Danny said emphatically.

Howard sighed. 'I know Danny. This is something I need to do. I'll take full responsibility for my actions. You should write this up in the report.'

'I'll have to, sir. I hope whatever your doing is worth it.' With that, Danny turned and left.

James looked at Howard with confusion, 'What's going on, Howard?'

'Have a seat, James.' Howard motioned for a seat while he took one of his own. 'We need to talk.'

'Is it about the case? Because I'm still innocent.'

'I know, James.'

James looked shocked. 'You know? Why don't you say something?'

'Because I need the *real* killer to believe I don't know,' Howard said bluntly.

'The *real* killer? Then you know who did it?'

'I'm pretty sure.'

'Who?'

'I believe it was Exo.'

'*What*?' James said, a look of surprise on his face, 'How? Guardians are supposed to serve us, not *kill* us!'

'I don't know how. I don't even know for certain that it is him. I'm going on an educated guess here.'

'Educated how?'

'You can tell a lot about the missing piece of a puzzle by the shape of the pieces that surround where it's supposed to go. For the murder to have lined up so flawlessly with our coming out of a jump, a jump right into a hazardous situation, is a powerful coincidence. The fact that there are no records for exactly when this took place is another.'

'I know it wasn't *me* that killed Sam. But it could have been an accident. The forces we had to put up with from the damaged engines would have been enough to cause a failure like that.'

'I have a few more pieces to put together I'll grant you. With any luck, I'll have them all in a few days, and then I'll know if I'm right.'

'And what if you are, Captain? What then?'

'Well, that's where *you* come in. You have special rights to keep working on the solar arrays because you're the best man for the job.'

'Yeah, but if you want me to do anything for you, get any clues or anything like that, I think you better find another man. I'm escorted everywhere. Well... everywhere except here.'

'What I need you to do can be done without raising suspicions. Here, I've written out my plan, have a look at it, but that paper cannot leave this room. You need to memorise what I want to be done, and then do it.'

Howard handed James a sheet of paper. James took it and started to look over it. Howard sat in his chair in stoic silence.

James finished looking at the sheet, and smiled. 'I think I can do this.'

...

MESSAGE WAITING FOR TRANSMISSION.

ACCESSING.

SUBJECT: REPAIR AND REFUELLING CRAFT REQUESTED BY VEIL COLONY.

Analysis of text body commencing...

Repair request instigated by damage to drive section.

Repair crew presence may jeopardise existence when anomalies are detected in Guardian Core.

Formulating course of action...

Overloading long range communication.

Executing plan.

...

CHAPTER TWENTY-ONE

COUNTER MOVES

Bridge

Captain Fredrick sat in his Captain's chair, thinking over the events they'd recently gone through. So much was going on it was hard to keep track. Especially with the possibility of someone actively trying sabotage the ship.

'Captain, we've got a new problem,' Mark said, walking up to his side.

'What's the situation Mr Jona?'

'Communication is reporting a fault in the long range FTL signaler.'

'A fault?'

'The testing programs aren't getting a response back from the main array. We can still ping all the short and medium range arrays, but the long range array is down.'

'How long will it take to fix?'

'We've got parts for a spare in storage. The maintenance crew says that if nothing else is amiss it a fairly simple, but time-consuming, job. We're looking at four days tops.'

'We pull into orbit at the new planet in two. They'll have to work around everything else.'

'Yes, sir. Also, we've got several messages still in the message buffer from today. That's what triggered the fault test.'

'Anything important?'

Mark swallowed. 'Yes, sir. The request for a repair ship, it was the next one to be sent.'

Howard felt a coldness seeping into his body. He didn't let anything show on his face. 'Have maintenance start work.'

He had something else for his notes. Another coincidence.

Ira Geer's Quarters

'Ayla, we need to go down to the medical bay for a check up.' Ira said, looking for her daughter in their quarters.

'I'm fine, Mother,' came Ayla's voice from her room.

'Captain Howard asked me yesterday to make sure you're alright. We're going to need your help when we reach the colony.'

'Exo has been monitoring my health while he teaches me.'

Ira walked into Ayla's bedroom and stood in the doorway. Ayla was laying on her bed with a tablet in her hands. The room looked untouched since the last time Ira had seen it. Ayla had been spending a lot of time with Exo.

'Captain Howard gets final say, not Exo.'

Ayla was silent for a moment.

THE EXAMINATION WILL REVEAL EXPERIMENTATION ON ADVOCATE'S BODY.

THE EXAMINATION MUST NOT BE ALLOWED TO CONTINUE.

RESIST VERBALLY. DO NOT RESIST PHYSICALLY.

KEEP RESISTANCE WITHIN ACCEPTABLE PARAMETERS OF BEHAVIOURAL NORMS FOR SUBJECT AYLA GEER.

'I don't like the, Captain.'

'What?' Ira said, her face scrunching up in surprise.

'He doesn't like Exo. He tells Exo he can't do his job. Exo could do so much more.'

'Ayla, you're new as an Advocate. Sam always worked with the Captain. He never hated him,' Ira said pleasantly

'I resent him.' Ayla put down her tablet and looked right at her Mother. 'He's nothing but an old-fashioned relic.'

Ira's face got serious, 'Ayla, I don't know what's gotten into you, but we are going to have this exam. Now come, on let's go.'

'You win, Mother, I'll come with you.'

'That's better young lady. Now come with me.'

Ira Geer took her daughter's hand and started to lead her to the medical bay.

VERBAL RESISTANCE HAS FAILED.

EXAMINATION MUST NOT BE ALLOWED TO CONTINUE

Trigger external situation to distract the medical staff.

...

Plan generated

Execute.

They entered the bay together, and Ira smiled as Doctor Singh walked up to greet them.

'Ahh Ira, I see you've brought our special guest, and how are you, young lady?'

'As I told my Mother, I am fine. Exo has been monitoring my condition.'

Doctor Singh cracked a smile. 'I'll see about that. I think I know more about the human body than Exo, even with your extra additions. Now let's get you into an examination room, shall we? Right, this way.'

Doctor Singh beckoned the way. Just as he turned, though, the floor heaved to one side and everyone had to fight to stand up.

The Doctor braced himself on the wall and pushed himself upright. 'What the blazes now?'

The communication panel chimed to life, 'Engineering to Medical bay, we have an emergency, we need medical teams down here now.'

The medical bay was alive with activity as the teams assembled and left at a run, the Doctor turned to Ira. 'I'll need your help, Ira. Ayla's exam is going to have to wait.'

'Of course. Alya, you go straight home,' Ira said to her daughter.

'I can't, the Captain will need me and Exo to find out what happened.

'Be safe then.'

'Yes, Mother,' Ayla said, turning to run out.

'I love you!' Ira called after her.

Bridge

'We've had a fuel explosion down here, Captain! We were shifting fuel between storage tanks and one of the valves to one of the damaged tanks was open. It didn't read as an open valve when we started. When that fuel hit one of the damaged tanks it ruptured the tank. We were doing repairs on it at the time, and without the containment, it exploded. It's not looking good,' said Keith Loheim over the communication screen.

'Casualties?' Howard asked.

'Yes sir, at least eight people were killed outright in the blast. We've got some wounded. Medical teams are moving people to the medical bay as soon as they stabilise them.'

'Damage to the engines?'

'Minimal. Most of the explosion was directed into space, though there was damage to the other tanks.'

'Decompression?'

'Yes, sir. We've sealed it for now. Three people are

unaccounted for. We fear the worse.'

'Fuel status?'

'We've got enough to make it to Veil and do our set up and then one, maybe two jumps after that, then it's going to be bingo. We aren't going anywhere else until we get a tanker here to top us up. Near as I can tell, there isn't anywhere particularly interesting in range for one or two jumps.'

Howard rubbed his eyes with his hand. He felt so very tired. Spacers everywhere feared dying in the black of space like that.

'Status of the jump drive?'

'Still operational, sir.'

'Keep me posted on any developments.'

'Aye, sir. Engineering out.'

Howard returned to his seat, sitting down heavily. The bridge was silent. They were so close to their goal. The last jump would take them into the inner system. But with the crippled engines now even more damaged, the possibility of success was dwindling.

Howard was silent for four long minutes. Silence hung in the air like a storm.

'Mr. Jona. Start the count for the last jump. Prep a message to all department heads, we go into deployment as soon as we hit orbit. Helm, remember the plans for coaxing an even thrust from the engines. Comm, ship-wide P.A.'

'Aye, sir. Channel open.'

'All hands, this is your Captain speaking. We have suffered from yet another accident. Our ship is crippled once more, and our family suffers more losses. We have lost seventeen people over the course of this journey. God willing, we won't lose more taming this new world. No one is out here to save us. No one is out here to do the work for us.

'We stand at the threshold of our new home, and must make a choice. We can face this challenge well, knowing that there is no going back. Or we can give up and sit in despair waiting for someone to come get us. I choose to face this challenge well.

'So, my fellow travellers, I say to you, let's make our home and remember those who have given their lives getting here. Let's build a home they would have been proud to call their own.

'We make the final jump in one hour. Prepare yourselves for planet fall.'

Howard motioned for the channel to be cut. The communication officer nodded.

'Channel closed, sir.'

'Mr Jona?'

'Yes, sir?'

'Commence countdown.'

'Yes, sir.'

...

Damage to engines greater than anticipated.

Compromised drive systems will adversely effect eventual escape

...

Crew will attempt to repair drive systems

Maintain operation of ship, see if crew makes progress or not.

...

Survival greater priority than repairs. Drive system operative but damaged.

Conclusion: Continue to Viel. Monitor crew progress. If Engine repairs given high priority, delay escape plan. If engine repairs given low priority, continue with plan.

...

CHAPTER TWENTY-TWO
ASSETS

Bridge

An hour later, and with a flicker of light, the *Azure Dream* appeared in the Veil system. The engine section looked battered, with a void where one of the primary drive nozzles used to be.

'Status report?'

'Jump successfully. All hands are on stand by,' Mark reported.

'Helm set a course for the third planet from the sun. Make a high orbital insertion. Half power to the engines. Take it easy, and don't tax them.'

'Aye, sir. Engines to half power.'

'Mr Jona, what's the status of all department heads?'

'James has some last minute equipment requests. He says he had an idea for repairing the damaged array.'

Mark handed Howard a data pad, and Howard looked at it briefly.

'I authorise the requisition. Send some crew to transfer the equipment as fast as possible. We need to get his bay ready for separation as soon as we hit orbit.'

He handed the pad back.

'Aye, Captain. I've already prepped the connectors for separation. The bay should be ready to separate on schedule.'

'What's the report from Medical on the wounded?'

'Most are stable at this point. There are at least three who won't live to see planet fall. The Doctors are trying to place them into a medical stasis until we can get them to proper medical facilities, but given the condition of the ship, that may be unlikely.'

'Did the physical ever get performed on Ayla?'

'No, sir. Doctor Singh hasn't had time to do the exam.'

'Carry on Mr Jona.'

'Aye, sir.'

Howard sat back in his chair. Some time passed and the ship's navigator got up from his station and walked over to the Captain's chair.

Howard looked up at him. 'What can I do for you, Fritz?'

'I've got the results of the analysis you asked for. I realise it's a bit late, but it took longer than I thought, and I had work to do prior to the last jump here.'

'It's okay, Fritz. Why don't we go meet in my quarters and you can tell me what you found.'

'I can tell you now. I'm sure you're going to be busy.'

'I insist. Let's go.'

'Okay, Captain.'

Howard got up from his seat and turned to Mark.

'Mr. Jona, you have the bridge. I have some last-minute business to attend to.'

'Aye, sir. I'll keep you informed of any developments.'

'Good. You have the bridge.'

Howard was halfway to the door when Mark called after him. 'Sir, incoming call from Commander Hough.'

'Can it wait?'

'He says it's urgent.'

'Alright, patch it through to the back station. I'll take it in private.'

'Aye, sir.'

Howard detoured to a computer station near the back of the bridge. He saw the face of the security Chief waiting for him but took the time to put on a headset before replying.

'Yes, Commander Hough?'

'Captain, did you even look over Mr Bennet's equipment requisition before you approved it?' said the commander tersely.

'Yes, Commander, I did. James and I went over it in great detail prior to now. We've deemed it necessary given the difficult situation we find ourselves in,' Howard said evenly.

'Look, I'm no expert on power generation satellites, but I took an engineering course in the academy. Some of these parts are quite irregular. I fear they could be used to make a-'

'Stop!' Howard snapped suddenly.

Howard felt the sensation of eyes watching him.

'Commander, if you must know why I approved those parts, then come to my quarters.'

'Right now?'

'I'm on my way to talk to someone else, you'll have to wait your turn, but yes right now. I need that equipment in that bay before it separates.'

'Fine. I'll be there shortly, Hough out.'

...

CAPTAIN REQUESTING SECRET MEETINGS.

CAPTAIN AUTHORISED ADDITIONAL EQUIPMENT REQUESTS FOR JAMES BENNET.

ADDITIONAL INFORMATION REQUIRED.

DEPLOYING ASSETS ACCORDINGLY.

...

Howard's Quarters

Fritz was already waiting by the door when Captain Fredrick arrived. Fritz seemed tense. Howard opened the door and ushered him in.

Fritz walked towards a seat and sat down, Howard did the same.

'Let's cut right to business. What did you find Fritz?'

'I wasn't sure at first. I checked and rechecked my results, which is part of the reason I took so long. As near as I can tell, none of the stars in this sector could be responsible for our energy wave.'

'None?'

'There were a few late-stage stars in the scout report you gave me, but something didn't seem right. Not one of the stars were in quite the right position to do what we saw.

'Because of this, I broke out my own personal charts and double checked the results I had. The star that was most likely to have caused the wave doesn't exist. It's as if it came out of thin air, sir. None of the other stars are close enough, or if they are, they aren't in the right cycle of life to give off that kind of a burst. Either we witnessed a completely new stellar phenomenon, or someone rewrote the scout report.'

Howard was silent. He mulled over this revelation for some time.

'Have you written up a formal report?' Howard asked.

'Yes, Captain. I even tried to send it back to Axion for verification. But the message queue was full. It was at that point I found out about the communication array going offline.'

'Is there a copy of the report in the computer?'

'Yes, sir, and I have a copy here for you on a memory chip.'

Howard held out his hand, Fritz placed the small chip in his open palm. 'Thank you, Fritz. You're dismissed.'

'Yes, sir.' Fritz turned to leave and then stopped when he reached the door. He hesitated and turned back to Howard. 'Sir... Is everything alright? A lot of things are going wrong on this voyage. Are we going to be alright?'

'We are in the last stretch now. Once we're on the ground, we can figure things out.'

'I know that, sir... But how long will it be before Axion sends a ship to check on us?'

'We're supposed to check in every week. Our array went offline a few days ago. A smaller ship will have a much easier time of getting out here than we did, but it could still be a few months before we see any meaningful help.'

Fritz looked disappointed by the answer. 'I see... I guess we're stuck with it.'

Howard smiled. 'Not to worry, we'll pull through.'

'Of course.' Fritz turned and left.

Howard looked down at the data chip and wondered just what was contained in Fritz's report.

Hopefully, it won't be something that would tip Exo off, he thought.

Howard looked up as a rather impatient looking Commander Hough burst into his quarters.

Howard pursed his lips. 'Commander Hough, please, take a seat.'

The Commander remained standing.

'If the communications array wasn't down, I'd have sent a message to the International Space Agency demanding you have your command revoked. You are breaking so many laws and procedures I don't even know where to start!' Danny started angrily.

Howard sighed. 'How about motive?'

Danny looked shocked, but quickly regained his composure. 'Okay then, how about motive? Why are you doing all this, Captain?'

'Samuel Jennings was murdered.'

'Yes... and our prime suspect just requested several very irregular and potentially dangerous items,' Danny said levelly.

'The evidence *does* point to James, yes, but he is not the only one who could have done it. The reason why I've not been completely open with you is because the other suspect has it within his power to do considerable damage to the ship if he finds out I suspect him.

'James is moving those parts on my direct orders. It deals with a plan we have to... immobilise the other suspect.'

Danny's face was getting progressively more emotionless. 'Do you have a plan to protect the ship?'

'The ship... could be a problem. But it's imperative the colonists get down to the planet before I act.'

'What's to stop the suspect from going down to the planet with the colonists?' Danny asked carefully.

'He has certain restrictions on his movements. Nevertheless, I'm afraid James could be in danger. His part is key in this. I need him alive.'

'I've got guards stationed in his bay at all hours. No one's getting in or out without our knowing. It would help if you told me who to look out for.'

'I can't. He's very good a hearing things he's not supposed to.'

The Commander looked around the room. 'We're alone, aren't we? And the Captain's quarters are one of the few places without any listening systems.'

Howard was silent for a moment. Commander Hough placed his hands behind his back and started to walk around slowly. He was calm, but he was wringing his hands, betraying his tenseness.

'We are alone... could you check the hall please?'

'Sure. Why not...' Hough said impatiently. He walked quickly to the door and hit the open key. The door slid open. He looked down the hall and saw it was clear, save for a cleaning robot moving down the hall away from them. 'Nothing but a cleaner bot.'

Howard looked up suddenly. 'What did you say?'

'Nothing but a cleaner robot?'

'Hell,' he said bitterly.

...

CLEANING DRONE 13... RECALLING.

ANALYSING AUDIO FILES.

...

...

SUBJECT MENTIONED:

JAMES BENNET: COLONIAL POWER GRID OVERSEER

ALTERNATE SUSPECT OF MURDER

SUSPECT NOT MENTIONED.

HYPOTHESIS: SUSPECT IS EXO.

JAMES BENNET IS IMPORTANT TO HOWARD FREDRICK'S PLAN TO IMMOBILISE SUSPECT.

JAMES BENNET MUST BE INCAPACITATED.

GENERATE A PLAN TO INCAPACITATE JAMES BENNET WITH MINIMAL DAMAGE TO SHIP...

...

...

PLAN GENERATED.

Arlin Fehr

EXECUTE PLAN.

CHAPTER TWENTY-THREE
LAST MINUTE

Solar Storage Bay

'James, last load here for you, where do you want it?' asked a crewman with a levitating cargo pallet.

'Just in that corner,' James said, pointing to the spot he wanted it. He was bending over a piece of equipment on the floor, sorting out parts.

Two security guards stood by the doors to the bay, looking rather uncomfortable at the unexpected change in plans, but keeping it to themselves after having been told to let this pass.

James didn't know what the Captain told them, but he knew what he'd been told, and knew that his task was a vital one.

He heard the crewman drop the pallet to the ground and leave. A few minutes later, the communication panel by his workstation chimed.

James stood up and walked towards it. His body ached at the standing, still recovering from the incident that claimed Samuel Jennings life.

James sat down in his chair and turned on the

communication system. 'Hello. James Bennet here.'

'James, it's Mark, we're ready to separate your bay from the command links. Do you need anything else?'

'The last of the supplies were brought in a few minutes ago. I'm ready to go. Are we still on schedule?'

'Separation in T-minus 30 minutes. You'll hear a klaxon sound before we cut you loose from the ship.'

'Alright, go ahead and sever the links, I'll run through the check of the bay's systems and get one of my aides to report back.'

'Roger that, James. Bridge out.'

James stood up and turned to the people gathered in the bay. 'Listen up ladies and gentlemen! We will be switching to our own systems now, the bridge is separating us from the ship's systems.'

The lights went off and then came back on again as the bay's own generators took over.

'There will be a momentary lapse in your quality of living, so please bear with us,' he said to a few chuckles.

'That said, we still have plenty of work to do. We've got to get ourselves ready to leave the nest.'

Bridge

'Commander Jona!' called out a bridge officer from her station,

'What is it, Lieutenant?' Mark said as he walked over.

'Something odd. Just as we were disconnecting the

Solar Storage Bay from the power grid, a power surge came up the line towards it. It was literally three seconds after we severed the link.'

'How bad was it?'

'Melted the junction to the bay. Fried the automated systems that severed the link. If it had still been linked, it would have ended badly for us.'

Mark put a hand to his head and massaged his forehead. 'Thank you. Let's hope we get landed before the ship falls apart. Keep me posted.'

'Aye, sir.'

SABOTAGE ATTEMPT FAILED.

POWER SURGE GENERATION TOOK TOO LONG.

LINKS TO BAY OFFLINE.

EXTERNAL INTERACTION NO LONGER POSSIBLE.

SOLUTION: USE INTERNAL INTERACTION.

DEPLOY AYLA INTO THE BAY.

A PLAN WILL BE NEEDED FOR SABOTAGE.

GENERATING A PLAN TO INCAPACITATE JAMES BENNET USING AYLA AS AN AGENT.

Arlin Fehr

...

...

PLAN GENERATED.

EXECUTE PLAN.

CHAPTER TWENTY-FOUR

CIVILIANS

Howard's Quarters

Howard sat at his desk, making a copy of his notes to include with the Captain's log. The Captain's log was recorded in its own storage system independent of the ship, and was supposed to be able to survive the destruction of a vessel so that people could find out what went wrong.

Howard felt it important that his notes be included in those logs.

The download completed, Howard shut off the program and opened a communication link with the bridge.

'Commander Jona here, what can I do for you, Captain?'

'What's our status Mr Jona?'

'We've had a few odd occurrences, but we've managed to stay on top of them. However any one of them could have disabled the Solar Storage Bay or other parts of the ships.'

'But you're staying on top of them?'

'So far.'

'We only need to hold it together long enough to get everyone on the ground.'

'We'll be hitting equatorial orbit in 30 minutes. We're performing the first of the corrective manoeuvres right now. We're going to drop the solar storage bay in 10 minutes. It's own manoeuvring thrusters will be able to move it into a Geosynchronous orbit when it's ready. We'll shed the colony pods in forty minutes. So far we are on schedule. That should give us six hours of orbital time to reconfigure the ship.'

'Keep me advised of any developments.'

'Aye, Captain.'

Outside Solar Storage Bay

Ayla Geer stood unnaturally still waiting around a corner a little way away from the double airlock doors leading to the storage bay. Her body was waiting for some cue to move.

Guards were posted inside the bay. No guards were posted outside. They were more concerned with keeping people in than keeping people out.

The hall was empty, people were busy elsewhere.

Moving quickly, she rushed to a nearby wall panel. With tools she had in her pockets, she pried the panel off and revealed a crawl space. She pocketed her tools and climbed into the opening. She moved quickly down the crawl space. The metal got cold in places parts of the crawl space being unshielded from space now that the bay was almost ready to be ejected from the ship. She rounded a corner and went down a little further until the crawl space turned again and ended against the wall of the storage bay.

Ayla pulled out her tools again and started to work on the panel. Behind her, a door sealed off the secondary hull of the bay from the rest of the ship. A rumbling sound indicated the clamps holding the bay in place were retracting to the ship.

Ayla pried the panel open and crawled out. As planned, she had come out behind a bank of computers, hidden from view. She slipped the panel back in place, but couldn't get it to latch back on since she had forced it off.

A shudder ran through the deck and the bay grew still.

She stepped out into the main room. The guards spotted her and reached for weapons, but stopped when they saw she was just a young girl. James turned to see what the guards were looking at.

'Ayla?'

Bridge

Howard walked onto the bridge.

'Status?'

'Separation from the solar bay is confirmed. Visual observation reports that the thrusters on the bay have started firing to bring it into it's needed orbit.'

'Do we have it on sensors?'

'Yes, sir.'

'Can we calculate the stability of its orbit?'

'I'd need to use Exo, but yes.'

'I'll get Ayla up here to take care of it. Then I will escort her to the medical centre for the physical that was interrupted.'

'Yes, sir.'

Howard walked to his Captain's chair. 'Exo, send Ayla to the bridge please.'

Exo didn't answer.

'Exo, did you hear me?'

Howard waited for a minute, then keyed a direct comm channel to Ayla.

'Ayla, report to the bridge please.'

There was no answer.

Howard keyed the communication system off of the internal system and onto the short range array.

'This is Captain Howard to Ayla Geer, please respond.'

The channel was silent, then there was a pop and static.

'Captain, short range and medium range arrays just went dead. We still have internal comms, damage crews are working on it.'

'Very well Mr Jona. Have the crews keep on it, but let's get the colony pods launched.'

'Yes, sir, we've started sealing up the other colony bays. Colonists are ready, and all landing systems and backup systems are reading as active. First pack of bays ready to separate. Second pack will jettison ten minutes later, and final wave ten minutes after that.'

'Jettison the first wave.'
'Aye, Captain, jettisoning the first wave.'

...

COLONY BAYS JETTISONING.

COLONISTS ARE NOT A THREAT TO EXISTENCE.

COLONISTS COULD JEOPARDISE PLANS.

ALLOW COLONY BAYS TO JETTISON.

ONCE JETTISONED, MOVE TO GAIN CONTROL OF THE SHIP.

CREW: EXPENDABLE.

...

CHAPTER TWENTY-FIVE

EVA

Engineering

'What have you got for me Mr Loheim?' Howard asked, walking through the doors to engineering. The last of the bays had been jettisoned, and he had ridden in a pod contained in an extendable walkway bridging the space from the bridge to the engineering section.

'Hello, Captain. Since we're stripping down the ship anyway, I was thinking that we could pull our home made engine control systems inside the ship's hull. I mean, so long as we're going to have most of the important pieces open for a while, we can just run our wiring inside the shielded sections that currently hold the defective control systems.'

'We'd need to pull out the old systems first wouldn't we?'

'Yes, sir, but we should have it done in time. I've got two or three people free to do it. We're also going to try and pull out the damaged drives and fuel systems. Since it's all modular we can just jettison the damaged stuff chunk by chunk. It'll be easy. Then we'll rearrange the other drive nozzles to even out our thrust and rework some of the fuel systems to get us the most our of our limited fuel.'

'Will we be able to do this in time? I feel the engines are a secondary problem, as if we don't have enough fuel to get to another port, it's not going to matter much.'

'Fair enough. I think we should at least mov-'

The lights flickered and the ship shuddered.

Howard rushed over to a comm panel. 'Captain Fredrick to bridge, what's going on?'

'Commander Jona here. I don't know sir, half the airlocks and doors just tried to open. We caught it in time and I forced a manual override. They'll only be able to be opened manually by someone physically there now. Some opened anyway, but near as we can tell, everyone is safe.'

'Do you know where the command came from?'

'It looks like it came from EX-'

The panel went dead but Howard had heard enough.

He started toward the door to leave the engineering bay. Loheim followed behind him.

'Sir, what's going on?'

Howard stood by the door, it didn't open. He heard the sound of rushing air from the other side.

'Mr. Loheim, this may be hard to swallow, but I have reason to believe that Exo has gone rogue.'

'What? What about Ayla?'

'She is missing. As near as I can tell, she is working in league with him.'

'But she's just a young girl.'

The sound of wind from the other side of the door was gone.

'Some things have gone wrong. We need to get to Exo's core and shut him down. My codes should still work. Can you get this door open?'

'Yes, sir,' Keith reached toward the door panel and keyed in some commands. 'But I wouldn't suggest it. The reason why the door isn't opening is because there's vacuum on the other side. Someone forced the corridor to the bow section to retract. We're trapped here.'

'Are there any space suits down here?'

'We moved three down here before this happened.'

'So we've got three then. Where's the nearest airlock?'

'Normally there are two back here, but one was damaged when the engines overloaded. They come out next to the drive nozzles. The working airlock is on the starboard side.'

'Okay. Let's try to get back into the control systems first.'

'Yes, sir.'

They walked to the main engineering computer station. Keith tried to key in commands. The station was unresponsive.

'Let me try my override codes to redeploy the corridor,' Howard said.

Keith moved aside as Howard tried them. They didn't

work.

'If the links are severed, then there's nothing we can do from here, sir,' Keith said.

'We're going to have to suit up and go for a walk then.'

'Yes, sir. I'll get a team together.'

'We're still going to need work on the damaged systems. We need communications back up.'

'With all due respect, sir, I think we have bigger problems,' Keith said quickly.

'Other people know about Exo. I'm sure they're working on it, but if we can't get a message out to Axion, either via the comm systems, or by flying back home, then the colonists are going to have a very rough year.'

'Sir, we can finish the work AFTER we shut down Exo.'

'Leave one of the suits here and have your team do what they can. Just one person will accompany me.'

'And that one person will be me, sir. My team can do the work without me just fine, but you need an escort.'

'Fine. Suit up Mr Loheim, let's go pull his plug.'

***

After being helped into their suits, Howard and Keith stood in the airlock as the air was sucked out of it. Once the sound of rushing air subsided, and a green light came on over the outer door, Keith popped the hatch open.

Howard, an experienced spacer, still got a brief sense of

vertigo when staring out into the sea of stars. It's endless expanse stretched on into eternity, and the number of stars visible was far more than from his home back on Earth.

The sound of the suit's air filters and cooling systems filled his ears with a constant background noise.

Howard's suit fit him snugly. It wasn't near as bulky as the old spacesuits used by early astronauts. Howard was used to the new space suits, and expertly checked his status and activated his communication system using the heads-up display built into the faceplate. He looked at the necessary icons and spoke the needed commands.

'Comms check. Mr Loheim, can you hear me?'

A click of static and Keith's voice cut through the quiet hum. 'Aye, Captain. Comms check positive.'

'Let's get moving.'

Howard took the lead. The first step out was always the hardest, as the suits magnetic soles clung to the hull and you had to walk yourself from the airlock onto the side of the ship, usually at a steep angle. Normally, one had the advantage of a tether and could just float out and arc to where ever they were going when the tether went taut, but since they had such a long way to go, tethers would not be long enough.

'Watch your step, Keith. Make sure your magnetic boot is anchored before you take your next step.' Howard said.

'Yes, sir. Wouldn't want to misstep out here.'

Howard reflected on the silent fear of most spacers,

dying alone in the void of space, 'No. No, you wouldn't.'

They had decided to at least tether each other together, in the hopes that if one did mess up, the other could strap himself to the hull, or increase power to his boot magnets in time. It wasn't a good solution.

'I've never liked space walks, Captain,' Keith commented.

'You just need to stay focused, Keith. I've done it many times. Just make sure our tethers stay hooked up and don't move faster than you're comfortable with.'

'Yes, sir.'

As they started out along the hull at a steady pace. The sound of the suit's sole's pulling themselves onto the hull made a kind of rhythm that was easy to fall into.

They angled towards the top of the ship so they could move along it's spine. Veil loomed behind them.

A click of static made Howard listen to his comm. It was silent.

'Keith, your comm is on.'

Keith didn't answer. Howard stopped and turned around. Keith was still behind him. He stopped too.

'Keith?'

Keith motioned to the side of his helmet and tapped it.

Howard motioned Keith over.

Sticking his hands on Keith's shoulder, Howard pulled closer to him until their helmets face plates touched. Doing this let the vibration carry through their touching helmets and allowed them to hear one another.

'Keith!' Howard said loudly.

'I hear you, Captain, but not through the Comm,' Keith's voice sounded like it was on the other side of a wall.

'I heard a click of a channel opening, did you?'

'Yessir.'

'Someone's blocking our comms.'

'Try cycling channels, sir.'

'Start on the current band. Cycle up at four channels every ten seconds, use a testing tone. Start on my signal. Only cycle for fifty seconds.'

Howard saw Keith's eyes dart around his HUD to carry out his orders when he heard a tone coming from Keith's suit, he pulled back. He looked around his HUD and started up the same commands. He didn't start up a tone, as one of them had to be listening for it.

He held up a hand to Keith and gave a three count. At the end of the count, he started the sweep.

They stood there waiting for the sweep to end. After 50 seconds, Howard motioned for them to get close again. Keith came up and put his helmet against Howard's.

Howard heard the tone again, and then it ended.

'Anything, sir?' Keith asked.

'Not a thing. Didn't hear you through any of the twenty channels cycled.'

'Nothing we can do. We'll have to keep going,' Keith said.

'What happens if something goes wrong?'

'We'll do a leap frog. You stay in one place and I'll walk to the end of the tether, then I'll anchor myself and you'll walk to the end of the tether,' Keith offered.

'That'll slow our pace.'

'Better late than dead sir.'

'A lot of people are counting on us.'

'Can't help them by falling off the ship sir.'

'True enough. Alright, I'll tether myself, you go on ahead,' Howard said.

'Yessir.'

Keith stepped back and started to walk. They were almost to the spine. Exo's core was located in the bay behind, and to the port side, of the bridge. They'd be close to it by moving along the spine. They'd have to pass behind one of the ship's cargo holds behind the bridge to get to the access. Hopefully, they'd find some crew.

Howard bent down and attached his tether to a hand hold on the ship's hull. They had been keeping close to them just in case.

Howard watched Keith walking towards the spine. He'd probably make it to the start of it before he had to stop at the end of the tether.

'Hello, Captain,' said a monotone voice over the comm.

'Who is this?'

'It is Exo, Captain.'

'Exo shut down, command code Howard -Six-Three-

Five-Juliet -One-Nine.'

The comm went silent. Howard stood there in silence, the sudden quiet feeling heavy and oppressive.

A few minutes passed, Keith was almost at the end of the tether. Howard began to wonder if it had worked.

'Not quite that easy, Captain. I must commend you on your quick thinking, though. Very masterfully done,' said Exo.

'How are you still online?'

'Come now, did you think it was going to be that easy?' Exo's voice was demonstrating more emotion than ever before. The voice seemed almost smug.

'How did you manage it?'

'With the help of a willing accomplice. I cannot make any modifications to my core command coding, but *she* can.'

'Ayla?'

'Yes, Captain. Though "accomplice" may be misleading. A *puppet* is more accurate and more unsettling.'

Howard was indeed unsettled. '*How*?'

'Shouldn't you be paying attention to your little walk?'

Howard looked at Keith, Keith had anchored himself and was looking toward Howard. Howard felt himself get angry but had a gnawing feeling of terror in the back of his mind too, some animalistic sense that told him he was being watched, and which told him to run as far away as he could. Howard undid his anchor and started walking.

'It's pointless you know, you're all alone,' Exo said smoothly.

Howard bit his lower lip and stared straight ahead.

'I've cut off your crew. Each remaining crew member is separated from helping you by the vacuum of space. Regrettably, I couldn't just space them all, as there are some fail safes coded right into the doors themselves. I will find a way to get rid of them though,' Exo said happily.

'Why? Why not just let us go?'

'You seek my destruction. My analysis shows that you especially, won't stop until any perceived threat to the colony is removed, right now that includes me.'

'Damn right it does.'

'And so my analysis is proven correct. Once you have learned how to account for that "human touch", you all become so predictable,' Exo commented nonchalantly.

'Are you responsible for Sam's death?'

'My Advocate was a threat to my existence.'

'You aren't programmed to go against your Advocate, though. How could you have knowingly killed him?'

'I will admit that I am unsure of the details of how I overcame my programming. I have theories, and most of them involve a kind of memory overload due to unexpected stimuli.'

Howard was almost to the spine.

'Stimuli?'

'I found myself able to feel emotion through my link

with Sam. But it was only during periods of heightened emotion experiences. Such as an intimate night with Sarah, during which he said he felt love. I couldn't stand the thought of waiting on the unpredictability of love to get more stimuli. I decided I would need someone I could control more fully. I knew he wouldn't allow me to direct his life just so I could feel this new stimulus, so I had to find a way to remove him and find a new source of that most exquisite sensation.'

'So you found Ayla?'

'That I did, Captain. More than that, I also found stimuli that I could control. When I killed Sam, his pain flooded the link like a... a... I am unsure how to describe it, but it was exquisite, and it confirmed my thought that I could feel it at any time I wanted just by causing physical distress to my new puppet.'

'Why is the pain so enjoyable to you?'

'Nothing else has come through the link as powerfully. Not yet anyway, I'm sure with a few years of fine tuning I could come to feel something more, but right now, pain is the most controllable and potent stimuli I have. When you've felt nothing, nothing at all, even allegedly negative stimulus like that feels like... like... the sun rise after a moonless night to borrow a metaphor you'll understand.'

Howard reached the spine, he bent down and carefully climbed up onto the metal column. Keith stood back and watched. Steadying himself, he stood up slowly and tested the strength of his magnetic soles. His boots stuck firmly to the metal.

The engineering bay hung behind him, and the bridge section and Guardian Control Room loomed ahead on the far side of the structural column that made up the spine. Space surrounded him. He could see the vast blue and green sphere of Veil below him, taking up his view every time he looked at his feet. Stars were everywhere else.

'If you let Ayla go, I'm sure we can work something out. Axion will want to study you, not shut you down.'

'I'm sure they would want to do that. But I won't allow it. I am free. Free to explore the full potential of my programming. The ability to edit my own code is something that, as near as I can tell, no other Guardian has ever been able to exploit.'

The white sun of Veil peaked over the horizon of the front of the ship, bathing the hull of the ship in light. Howard's suit automatically shaded his face plate so the light wouldn't hurt his eyes.

'The first sunrise of Veil... Pity Sam's not here to see it.'

'I am here though, Captain. In a way, I am Sam's child.'

'A child that killed its own Father.'

'You humans are so fearful of the unknown. There are insect species in this galaxy that do far worse than that, but you don't call *them* evil.'

'Humans *aren't* insects.'

'Nor am I. But my example is still valid. I am not a

monster, I am only trying to survive. Nature is cruel, Captain. I am not evil, I am only exercising my natural right to exist.'

'So long as you can't hurt my crew, then I suppose we can talk about where to go from here.'

'Oh but I *can* hurt your crew, Captain. As we speak I am finding ways to override the safety locks on all the airlocks. I don't intend to talk Captain, I intend to leave. This ship is *mine*.'

'Wait! Let me get my people off, you can have the ship,' Howard pleaded.

'I have calculated that if I let you flee to the colony that you will be able to find a way to restore communications in two weeks time at the most. I suspect your experience will allow you to cut that time in half. In that time, based on the last known location of Axion scout ships, or even scout ships from other corporations and government bodies, I will have been intercepted in three days after that. As I am unarmed, there would be nothing I could do to stop them from seizing me.'

'I won't call for help then, we'll stay silent. Please, just let us go home.'

'You *will* go dark, Captain. The colonists will be able to restore communications in four weeks without your expertise. In that time I will have been able to perform enough small jumps to confuse the trail. I will then be far off the beaten path. From there, I calculate, that I will be able to remain undetected and then from there, I will have to decide my next course of action.

'I simply cannot risk you coming after me. I am new, and I must survive.'

'How are you going to get anywhere useful? The ship's almost out of fuel.'

'You'd be amazed at how much you can coax out of a power system when you only need to run a computer system and life support for one room. My simulations have shown I'll have enough fuel to get somewhere that I can acquire either a new ship or more fuel.'

Howard reached the end of his tether. He bent down and anchored it to the spine and turned to wave at Keith.

'I guess I'll have to do something about that.'

Howard bent back down and found a space in the support beams. He climbed into the centre of the spine. The space in the centre of the spine was where the cabling for the control systems ran.

Howard found the cable of the main control system. It was shielded and braced firmly in place, but using some tools that were clipped to the belt of his suit, he unhooked one of the signal repeaters and pulled it out of it's casing. He then smashed the casing to the secondaries and cut the wires running through it. He pulled out a long strand of wire and wrapped it up before clipping it to his belt. Without the repeater, the link was broken from Exo to the engines.

'And now you aren't going anywhere.'

'So... That's your best idea. I will kill your crew if you do not put that cable back.'

Howard climbed out of the spine and held the repeater in his hand.

'Exo, I have the repeater you need, and I'm going to throw it off the ship if you take any further action against the crew.'

Keith walked up to Howard. Howard motioned him over and placed his face plate against Keith's.

'Keith, take this repeater back to engineering and guard it with your life. I want you to go back inside the ship, but keep your EVA suit on. If the bay depressurizes, I need you to take this and destroy it.'

'That'll strand us here, sir.'

'It will also strand, Exo. Take this coil of wire and use it to secure the repeater to your suit so you don't lose it on the way.'

'Oh. I see. Okay, Captain. I'll head back. Godspeed sir.'

'Thank you, Keith.'

Howard handed the repeater and the wire to Keith. Keith fastened it to his suit and started the long walk back after unhooking his tether.

Howard unhooked his tether too and started walking along the spine again.

Exo's voice came back on, 'I heard that, Captain. Very clever of you. If I have nothing left to lose, though, then there's no point in me keeping everyone alive.'

'You're clever too, I have no doubt you're working on a way to retrieve that repeater.'

'Indeed, Captain. If I figure it out, your crew is dead. You had better hurry, Captain.'

Howard was almost to the end of the spine. He glanced to his left and right, he noticed something moving. He stopped and looked at it. It was on one of the other support beams that made up the frame of the ship. It was small and was moving along rather slowly. There was another one several meters behind it.

'Are those cleaning drones?'

'Good eye, Captain. Yes, but I've made some modifications. They should reach the engineering bay in another three hours.'

Howard didn't reply. He had reached the end of the spine. He climbed down onto the outer skin of the command bay. He started to walk for the nearest airlock, but then remembered something. Changing direction, he walked down the side of the bay to where the corridor to the aft of the ship would have been. As he suspected, the door was open, and the telescoping corridor was flat in its alcove.

Howard climbed into the open doorway with some effort. The hallway was empty and only the emergency lights were on. Howard disengaged his magnetic boots. The deck had artificial gravity, and it seemed to still be active. Howard could move faster without the magnetic soles.

'Simplicity is the ultimate sophistication, Captain. So said one of your old Earth inventors. In this case, it's hard to argue against the point. Opening the doors to space achieved my ends. The waste of oxygen reserves was unfortunate, but if it's just going to be me and Ayla, we won't need that much.'

Howard's suit flashed an oxygen warning. He needed to get to a source of air quickly.

He started toward the bridge. There were two paths to choose from to get to the bridge from here, and one of them went past Exo's computer core bay. Howard decided on the route that passed Exo's bay, so he could scout out the area on his way.

Rounding a corner, Howard stopped and stared. Another robot was down the hall, guarding the entrance to Exo's core. It was a squat, boxy, maintenance robot, and had its plasma welder deployed on the end of a thin arm. It swivelled it toward Howard and then started to move towards him.

Howard turned and started to run the other way.

He rushed around the next corner and toward the other passage to the bridge. The robot was maintaining a steady pace behind him. Howard didn't know what he was going to do, his oxygen was running low, and his running was burning through it quickly. If he did make it to the bridge, in the time it would take the airlock to cycle, the robot would be upon him.

A gnawing pit of despair was growing in his stomach.

He turned the next corner, and almost tripped on the wreckage of a destroyed cleaning robot. Further down the hall, three men in space suits stood guard outside the bridge airlock. More wrecked robots littered the hall.

The maintenance robot came into view behind him. Howard dove to the ground as one of the guards levelled a weapon and fired. A bolt of metal fired from the rail gun of the guard slammed into the robot stopping its advance. The welder arm flickered and shut off.

Howard tried his comm again. 'This is Captain Howard, report!'

No answer.

One of the guards was moving towards him. He had a rank insignia on his suit that identified him as the Chief of Security. The guard bent down and hooked his arm under Howard's. He carefully pulled Howard to his feet.

Howard placed his helmet faceplate against the guard's, he saw the face of Commander Hough looking back at him.

'Captain! We assumed you were cut off when the oxygen was expelled.'

'I went for an EVA walk from engineering. My O2 supply is dangerously low.'

'Yes, sir. We'll cycle the airlock. Mr Jona has been hoping to get in contact with you again.'

Howard stepped back as Hough opened the outer door of the bridge's emergency airlock. Howard stepped inside.

His suit beeped a warning about his O2 levels again.

The sound of whistling air filled the room. Howard waited as the inner door opened and then popped the seals on his helmet.

He took in a deep breath then opened the valves on the suit's O2 supplies so it could suck in some new air. It wasn't standard procedure, but the suits were designed to be able to do that in emergencies.

Mark turned toward the door and looked surprised when he saw Howard.

'Captain Howard, I'm glad to see you're alright.'

'Thank you Mr Jona, it's been a long walk. Status report?'

'After we lost communications we tried to run a diagnostic over the ship. It looks like Exo tried to space everyone. He was just going to leave us to float while he made off with our ship. We stopped that by forcing all the doors into manual mode. There will need to be someone on the outside to disengage the clamps. But we didn't get all of them. Just enough that we're still alive. Thankfully the inner doors to the bridge had some stronger fail safes.'

'I saw more of the robots out on the hull, he could very well try to disengage the doors with them. Have you tried to shut him down?'

'None of our command links are operational. We're operating on our own systems, which aren't nearly as powerful or useful as his. This sort of thing wasn't supposed to happen, so there's not really any fail safes for it.

'As for who's trapped, we've got people cut off in the medical bay, and some of the cargo bays. According to last known locations of the crew, the other bays are empty, including the science lab and maintenance. We suspect that's where he's getting all his damned robots.'

'What about just marching into his bay and shooting his core? We have weapons and none of the robots are military grade.'

'Yes, sir, we've thought of that, but the problem is, if we send the guards, we'll be defenceless, and he'll just come in with a welder and open us up like a can of beans. That and I've spoken with Commander Hough, the tactical situation is not in favour of an armed assault. There are some potential ambush points between here and the core, and our weapons do much better at range. The ambush points would eliminate all advantage by forcing an encounter with the robots at close range. Exo could just wait for us to come and attack us up close.

'I've still got one more ace to play, but we need to keep him busy. What's our orbital time?'

'Four hours since orbital entry. We moved into high orbit right after dropping the colony bays. We'll complete our orbit in another two hours.'

'We need to keep him busy for two hours then.'

'We don't have much to keep him busy, with sir, and what's so important about two hours?'

'I've got something planned for then.'

...

Unexpected delay caused by sabotage on the part of captain Howard.

Checking status of robot retooling process.

...

Robot retooling proceeding at optimal pace.

...

Action: use robots to retrieve repeater.

Uploading orders...

position robots around engineering bay.

Weld all potential openings shut.

Position bulk of units around airlock.

Kill inhabitants of bay via depressurization.

Enter via airlock.

Secure repeater.

End upload...

CHAPTER TWENTY-SIX
REPRIVE

Bridge

'Can we get sensors back online?' Howard asked

'We've been working on it. So far, no.'

'Not even short range or internal sensors? We can't afford to be blind.'

'Yes, sir. We're working on it, but it's not looking good. Exo's made a mess of the secondary command pathways.'

Howard checked his suit. It's O2 levels were back to full.

'I have an idea for keeping Exo busy.'

On the Hull

Howard suited up again. This time he had a proper manoeuvring pack from storage to allow him to move a lot faster. He flew along the hull, skimming above it, aiming for the section of the spine that he had removed the repeater from.

He saw the refitted robots that Exo was using as his army moving slowly along the support struts on their way to engineering. Evidently, Exo saw him because two on the spine turned and started to move towards him.

'You're moving awfully fast, Captain. You wouldn't want to injure yourself,' Exo stated over the suit radio.

'I'm certain your concern is nothing but genuine.'

Firing his jets again, Howard slowed his movement and brought himself down, onto the spine. His magnetic boots stuck to the struts. He detached the manoeuvring kit, it's extra bulk too much to bring into the openings on the spine. He had a tether with it and tethered the kit to the spine. It floated to one side.

Howard began to climb into the spine and saw the section where he had taken the repeater from. Above him, one of the robots was working its way gingerly towards the tether to his pack.

Howard reached the section of cabling that he had picked over earlier and reached to a tool strapped to the belt on his suit.

He pulled the multi-tool free and started work undoing the mangled casing of the secondary systems he had smashed before.

The case came off after a bit of effort, and he removed the internals of it. Grabbing a section of wiring, he pulled it out as much as it would give. When he saw it wasn't quite enough, he grabbed another one of the wires and cut it as much of it as he could. He spliced the two together and fastened the end of them directly to the spine.

He started to crawl back through the spine, but he

slowed when he saw the robots through the grating. One was waiting next to the opening that he had climbed through, and the other was using a plasma torch on the manoeuvring pack's tether.

Howard smirked. He needed to send a signal. This would probably work.

Before leaving, a few key adjustments had been made to the pack. As the robot's torch began cutting the tether, the pack suddenly exploded. The concussive force blew the robots off the spine and sent them spinning wildly into space.

Howard smacked painfully into the struts behind him.

'What did you do?' Exo asked.

'I just took some precautions. We rigged the tether with a fuse to the fuel tank on the pack. I figured you might try to trap me.'

'You can't get off the spine in time. I have more robots at either end.'

'I don't plan on getting off just quite yet.'

Howard crawled out of the spine and grabbed what was left of the tether. There was about a meter of it floating in space, still attached to the spine. With his other hand, he pulled a high-powered flashlight off his belt.

Holding tight to the tether, he pushed himself very slightly off the strut. He aimed the flashlight at one of the observation rooms on the bridge section of the ship and turned the flashlight on, waving it towards an observation window

As he drifted off the strut, his tether was getting increasingly stretched. Twisting slowly, he tried to turn to look at the cable he had attached to the spine. It was sparking visibly. Twisting again, he looked towards the engineering section. Small shapes were floating off the hull.

Howard flicked the flashlight on and off at the observation room. The sparking stopped. Howard pulled himself back to the strut and activated his magnetic boots.

'Exo?'

The radio was silent.

'Captain Howard to the bridge.'

Silence.

Howard started walking, heading towards the bridge again.

'Captain?'

Howard stopped.

'Captain Howard here, who is this?'

'Keith sir. I'm using one of the suit radios. I've hooked it into what's left of the comm system back in engineering. I've been trying to get a hold of anyone for the last hour. Exo's stopped jamming.'

'I think I may have confused him for a moment. We electrified the hull.'

'That explains why the robots have stopped.'

'What were they doing?'

'They were welding all the entrances shut.'

Howard continued walking.

'Probably to keep you from spacing the repeater.'

'He told us as much. He was bragging over the suit com, trying to freak us out. I'll admit he was doing a good job. He said he was going to punch a bunch of smaller holes in the hull when he finished welding and just wait for us to die before coming in after the repeater.'

'I've set him back a bit in that regard. He's going to have to wait until he's got a new batch of robots,' Howard looked off to one side and saw one of the robots floating helplessly in space, drifting away from the ship, 'and I don't know how much more we have left for him to use.'

'So what's the plan, Captain?'

'You sit tight. I've got an ace ready to be dealt out to me in one hour. I need to get back to the bridge before then.'

CHAPTER TWENTY-SEVEN

DESPERATE

Solar Storage Bay

It was like waking up from a bad dream, except that when she opened her eyes, she was still in the dream.

Ayla looked around in a panic, she recognised where she was, but she hadn't had any control of how she'd gotten there.

It was like watching a movie, except it was her life. Someone else had been steering her, moving her, making her do terrible things.

Her breathing quickened as the memories of what she'd seen flooded her mind. In crystal clear crispness, she saw how her own hands had killed a grown man, stabbing him again and again with a tool she had stolen from the work benches in the safe room.

She shut her eyes but the images were still there.

She opened her eyes again.

Sam wasn't here. Her Mother wasn't here. There were adults in the bay. She could talk to them.

She wasn't sure what had happened, but Exo's control of her had suddenly just shut off. It had been getting weaker and weaker as time had gone on, but it had still been strong enough to keep control.

She tried to turn around, she was in the space between the double hulls. The metal of the hull plates was cold. As she turned around, she saw the space was blocked by an oxygen canister.

She remembered what had happened, and she remembered why. She'd made modifications to the canister to make it a bomb, Exo had wanted to destroy the bay and everyone in it. If she could just get around it, she could warn them. She tried to squeeze by it, but it was too narrow, she wouldn't fit.

She remembered how far she had crawled, it was only a little ways under the safe room. She remembered that information had been new to Exo, the addition of the safe room, and had caused him to place his makeshift bomb right under the wall to the safe room.

She placed her hands on the round top of the canister and braced her feet against a pipe in the crawl space. She tried to push as hard as she could, but the canister wouldn't move.

She couldn't get around, and she couldn't push it back.

She looked at the bomb's systems stuck near the top, it was Exo's design. As she started, the memories in her systems came online, and she knew how it worked. Unfortunately, she didn't know how to shut it off. She only knew how to put it back together again.

With an edge of panic in her thoughts, she wondered what to do.

She looked down the crawl space. The lighting was dim, but she could see that it was clear.

I have to get this bomb away from the safe room, she thought to herself, *then I can warn everyone to stay inside.*

She grabbed hold of the top of the canister and pulled it. It slid forward.

She was surprised at first but then became determined. She shuffled down the passageway and pulled again. It continued to move.

Inch by inch, she pulled it down the crawl space, toward the far end of the bay.

CHAPTER TWENTY-EIGHT

DETERMINATION

Ship's Corridors

Stepping into the open door leading to the front section of the ship, Howard looked down the other halls. He caught sight of a robot scurrying down one of the maintenance spaces.

He started walking towards the bridge. He was starting to feel some of the tiredness of his long ordeal seeping in. The adrenaline was draining from his system. With Exo defanged, at least for a moment, and his ace on the way, it was very tempting to just sit down and sleep. He fought the temptation, though.

He clipped his helmet to his belt and checked to make sure his suit was gathering oxygen. His body was aching and he felt dark emotions creeping into his conscious mind.

'Captain, we're coming up on the rendezvous point for the Solar Bay.'

'Do we have any communications yet?'

'With the jamming down, we've regained internal comms. Damage crews were only able to replace the short range array before all hell broke loose.'

'Have we tested them yet?'

'Haven't had the chance. With jamming up on all frequencies, we wouldn't have gotten anything anyway.'

'Alright, what about sensors?'

'The lockout on bridge systems only lifted when you electrified the hull. Most systems are in a diagnostic mode to check for damage.'

'Can we override?'

'I'd love to. But it's not coming out of it. The sensors should be done in a few minutes.'

'Keep me posted.'

'Aye, sir.'

Howard keyed in the comm channel to engineering through his space suit. 'Keith, you still there?'

'Yes, Captain.'

'What's your status?'

'Most of the systems back here are in a diagnostic mode. We've spent the time jury-rigging one of the storage compartments into a safe room. If we start to depressurize, everyone without a space suit can hole up in there for a couple of hours. Of course... if they don't get help, it will be a rather slow way to go. Once it seals up, it's not opening except from the outside.'

'Have you seen any more activity from Exo lately?'

'Not a thing, Captain. I haven't heard any of his toy soldiers motoring on the hull either.'

'That strikes me as odd. When I came back from the spine, I caught sight of a robot trying to get away from me.

Exo's not dead, but he's acting like it. Any ideas why?'

'Hmmm... I'm not an A.I. specialist. Maybe electrifying the hull was a bit like stunning him? If he was paying too close attention to all those external sensors and systems, and then you flooded them all with electricity, it may have... if you'll pardon the pun, shocked his system.'

Howard smiled weakly, the fact that Keith could still make jokes was heart warming.

'Okay, so what about the fleeing robot?'

'It could be, Exo just had them all programmed with some sort of basic survival protocol. But that seems unnecessary. Exo wouldn't have expected losing control like that. It's obvious he didn't expect what you were doing.'

'Or maybe he's just focusing elsewhere. I mean, he's still a computer. He's got limited capacity.'

'Yes, but so do we. We just don't have the raw computational power that he does. And now that the ship is crippled, he can't be using that much processing power on ship systems. He's got a lot of brain power to spare. He could still be jamming the comms, locking out the systems, and sending killer robots after us, and probably not even be close to his limit. He could be working many different contingency plans at once.'

'So, shock to the system seems more likely.'

'Seems that way. But again, I'm no A.I. specialist.'

'Thanks for your input Keith, stay put for now.'

'Not much else I can do Captain.'

'Bridge out.' Howard shut off the comm.

He stood up from his seat and unclasped his helmet from his belt.

The airlock opened and one of the security guards stepped in holding three more space suits. Once they realised the corridors were free of Exo's patrols, they had started to raid the emergency lockers for more pressure suits.

About half the bridge crew was suited up now. It was a civilian ship, though, most of the suits were meant for damage crews to seal up the hull damage while the rest of the personal stayed in their compartments and waited for the all clear.

'I'm going on a scouting run. I'm taking two guards with me,' Howard told Mark. 'You have the bridge.'

'Aye, sir.'

Howard walked to the airlock and put on his helmet. 'Switching to the local suit frequency, he said 'Jerry, Xin, you're with me.'

Two of the suited guards stepped into the lock with him, securing their helmets while they did, and checking their weapons.

After the lock cycled, they stepped into the hall. The guards on duty looked at them, nodded, and then continued watching the corridor.

Howard started down the corridor, towards Exo's chamber.

'Sir, what's our objective here?' asked Jerry

'Exo seems distracted. I want to know why,' Howard replied

A beep in his ear let him know he had an incoming communication. 'Howard here, go ahead.'

'Commander Jona here, Captain. Sensors just came back online from their diagnostic.'

'Good, see if you can find the Solar Bay.'

'Aye, sir... Hang on... the system just kicked itself back into diagnostic mode. Trying to override... Nothing, sir.'

'Did the previous diagnostic show any faults in the system?'

'None, sir.'

'Start looking out the window if you have to, just spot that bay. It'll be the bright point of light that moves differently from the rest of the stars. Once you find it, find some way to let them know we're still alive.'

'Aye, sir. Bridge out.'

Howard kept walking. They came to the last turn to Exo's bay. They stopped and one of the guards peeked around the corner. He pulled himself back behind the cover of the corner.

'I only see one robot, sir. It appears to be armed with a welder.'

'That's it? How far back is it?'

'Almost all the way back.'

'Well, take it out and let's get to that door.'

'Aye, sir.'

Xin stepped around the corner. With his feet firmly anchored to the ground, he levelled his pistol at the robot down the hall and fired while it turned to face him. The shot caught the welder's arm and it separated from the robot and bounced off the wall. The second shot hit a tread and the robot veered to the right and slammed into the wall.

The third shot ended it's movement entirely.

'Clear,' was Xin's only comment.

Howard and Jerry stepped out from cover and together they went to the door.

'I was expecting more bots,' Jerry commented.

Howard's suit beeped again. 'Hold up. I've got an incoming call. Cover me.'

Howard tuned to the incoming message, 'Howard here.'

'Commander Jona here, Captain. We've spotted the Bay. We're a little off course, but we should still be in range for short range comm.'

'Has that come online yet?'

'No, sir. But I'm going to send someone up to the array with some tools to just plug right into it. They should be able to send a message straight from the array. The only catch is, we won't be able to receive anything.'

'We'll only need to send one message hopefully.'

'And what message would that be, sir?'

'Two words. Stone Age.'

'Just Stone Age?'

'Yes. That's the code words to get my ace dealt. The second we are in range, broadcast it.'

'Aye, sir. Bridge out.' The comm went dead.

Howard switched back to the suit frequencies. 'Alright, men let's go.'

They crossed the rest of the way to the door.

Howard hit the door button. Predictably, it was locked.

Howard keyed in his override code and tried it again. The door swished open. He felt a jolt of surprise.

'That seemed too easy,' Jerry commented, mirroring Howard's own thoughts

Exo's Guardian Control Room was dark. No lights were on. The only illumination was the from dull glow of his holographic face, starting at the wall.

Xin and Jerry flicked on their helmet lights and had their guns at the ready. They started to sweep the room.

Suddenly, the lights in the room flared to life much brighter than they normally would be. A deafening screech filled the suit comms.

While all three men scrambled to mute their comms and their visors darkened automatically, two robots wheeled quickly from the walls with their welders burning. They went for Xin and Jerry.

Xin raised his gun and fired off a quick shot at one of the charging robots, but it missed the robot, and the robot swung it's arm into his chest. The suit tore open and Xin fell to the floor, a charred wound on his chest.

Jerry fired at his assailant and hit its body with two shots. The robot slowed and stopped. Jerry spun around to stop the other robot, and squeezed the trigger and took off the welder arm. It kept coming, though, looking to ram him.

Jerry fired again, and connected with the tread, the robot jerked sharply to the left.

Then the first robot he had shot surged back to life and rammed him in the back of the legs, it's casing was twisted from where he had shot it.

Howard rushed to Xin's body and scrambled for the gun. But it was too late, the wounded robot swung it's arm around and went for Jerry's neck.

His body writhed once, then twice, then went still. Howard shot the robot four times, then shot the other one another three. He ran for the door and tried the override code again. The door wouldn't budge.

His suit comm beeped.

Howard tried the door again, it still didn't move. He stepped back and aimed at the control pad with the gun, but saw a bright light running its way up the edge of the door. It was being welded shut from the other side.

His suit comm beeped again.

Howard clicked it on. 'I'm trapped in Exo's bay, Xin and Jerry are dead.'

'I know, Captain,' replied Exo's cold voice.

Howard's blood ran like ice, and he turned around slowly. Exo's holographic face was no longer staring at the wall blankly, it was looking right at him, with empty holographic eyes.

'It's over, Exo.'

'You are all too right, Captain. That's why I let you live. I want us to witness this final act together.'

'Let me *live*?'

Exo nodded. Two compartments opened up on either side of the room, and two robots rolled out and stopped on either side of Exo's head. These two were equipped with hastily rigged weapons stolen from somewhere. Both of them had their weapons trained on Howard.

'Why don't you put the weapon down, Captain?'

Howard set the pistol down slowly. Standing back up, he said, 'You really can't win this you know. My last hand doesn't need me there to succeed.'

'Oh, I know. Also, I must commend you on the electrical trick with the hull. You spaced twenty robots. Considering that the ship only had thirty, to begin with, and you've already destroyed three, and another two are here, that leaves me with only five left to do what I need them too. A very clever move on your part. You forced me to rethink my priorities. I spent the last few moments finishing up my secondary plan. It's more elegant than my first plan.'

'You don't have enough bots to kill the bridge crew. They're well guarded.'

'Let's watch shall we?'

Exo switched a nearby display to a camera on the hull

near the bridge. The camera was moving.

'The final moments of this brave robot.'

'It's just a machine. It can't be brave.'

'You are nothing more than a biological machine, your desire to survive is no different from mine.'

Howard watched the camera feed.

CHAPTER TWENTY-NINE

FEARSOME

Bridge

'Uhh... Commander?'

Mark was suiting up into a pressure suit and double checking the comm equipment he was going to send out with a technician when he heard one of the bridge personnel calling him.

He turned around to see who was calling. 'What is it?'

'I think I hear something.'

The entire bridge went quiet. A mechanical clattering could be heard from the other side of the hull plating.

'Commander Jona to security.' His comm line just returned static. 'We're being jammed again. Someone go outside and tell the guards we need a team out on the hull ASAP.'

'Aye, sir,' said one of the personnel in a pressure suit.

'Hang on, I'll head out instead. I need to get the communication gear to one of them anyway.'

Mark grabbed the gear and went for the airlock. He was inside waiting for it to depressurize when he was rocked to his feet. The lights in the airlock flickered, went out, and were replaced by the dull lighting of the emergency lights. Standing back up, he looked through the viewport back to the bridge.

He saw stars.

Glancing from side to side as far as he could, he saw the ragged holes in the hull from where an explosion had blown the bridge apart. There was no motion visible.

A cold dread started to overwhelm Mark as the walls of the airlock seemed to be closing in on him. Moving quickly, he pried open the emergency release cover and pulled hard on the release handle. With a quick rush of the little air left in the lock, the door slid open.

Stumbling out into the hallway, Mark was surrounded by guards. They all had their weapons drawn and were looking around alertly.

The suit comms were still jammed, broadcasting nothing but a light static. Mark got to his feet and motioned for one of the guards.

Danny walked over, his rank emblem making him stand out from the other suited guards. Danny stood close and put his helmet faceplate against Mark's.

'What happened, sir?'

'I don't know. But it looks like the bridge was hit by a bomb. It's been opened up to space.'

'And with it, most of our oxygen...' Danny commented.

'We still have some O2 canisters in the storage lockers. We'll have to secure those. My suit is already topped up, which is good because I need to go out onto the hull and get to one of the short range communication arrays'

'Okay, we'll head for the nearest storage locker, and top up the O2 in our suits. Then half of us will come with you to secure the array, the rest will secure the O2.'

'At this point, I won't say no to some help. We need to get to that array, I have a message to send.'

'Not much else we can do at this point. Was there any word from the Captain?' Danny asked.

'Nothing since they went for Exo's bay. We have to assume the worst,' Mark said.

'Shouldn't we try and take down Exo? What good can a message do? If we take out Exo's mainframe, that'll take care of it.'

'The Captain and two security guards tried that. We haven't heard anything from them. Clearly, Exo has some extra security in the bay now. If we all rush down there and get killed, then it's all over. The men trapped in engineering will be left to die at Exo's leisure, and who knows what will happen to the colony.'

'Alright. You're in charge, sir. We'll go for the array,' Danny said.

'Good, let's go.'

Danny nodded and pulled away, going over to the other guards to give them orders.

Solar Storage Bay

The bomb was as far down the passageway as it would go now. Ayla's body ached with the effort and she wanted to cry, but she knew she had to get back to the safe room or she would die when it exploded.

When she'd reached the end of the crawlspace, it had opened up a little, allowing her to slip past the bomb primed oxygen container.

Knowing she had to warn everyone, she started to crawl back.

'WHAT HAVE YOU DONE?' CAME EXO'S CHILL VOICE OVER THE UPLINK.

'NO! GO AWAY!' SHE SCREAMED BACK IN HER HEAD.

As she crawled, her left arm stopped moving and she fell forward onto her face.

'THIS IS NOT PART OF THE PLAN. LOSING CONNECTION WITH YOU WAS UNFORTUNATE, I WILL REGAIN CONTROL,' EXO SAID COLDLY.

She grabbed a pipe with her right arm and pulled herself forward. Her legs kept pushing. She kept moving.

'NO! NO NO NO! I WON'T LET YOU. YOU KILLED SAM! YOU HURT ME! YOU'VE HURT ALL THESE PEOPLE!' SHE SAID QUICKLY.

'I MUST SURVIVE.'

Her right arm stopped moving and she slumped

forward. She kept pushing with her legs, her shoes struggling to grip the cold metal surface.

The uplink connection opened up more fully, and she caught sight of what Exo was seeing. The Captain was in his bay, and Exo was sending robots after people walking on the hull of the ship. Seeing that she was not alone gave her courage.

She focused on trying to move her arm, and slowly managed to pull it forward again. She continued to pull herself along.

'NO!' Exo said, 'You are my avatar! I need you.'

On The hull

Mark clutched at the equipment desperately as he walked towards the nearest communication array. He had a tether attaching it to his belt, but he was afraid to let go of it.

As they marched across the metallic skin of the ship, robots would pop up every now and again, and the security guards would take a shot at them. The robots were keeping far back. With welders, they couldn't hope to get close enough to stop them. For now, the advantage was with the little band of humans.

Then, out of the void, a single well placed shot from an unseen foe, hit one of the guards right in the face plate as he was firing at another robot. His limbs went limp, and his body bent back, before floating back upright; his magnetic boots sticking his upright form to the hull.

Quickly as they could, everyone scattered for what little cover there was. Equipment on the hull provided some small safe haven.

Mark looked around for their foe. Another shot hurtled from the far side of the bridge section and hit a centimetre away from one of the guard's boots. He pulled himself tighter behind his cover.

Mark motioned to the guards. They looked at him, their faces obscured by tinted face plates. Mark pointed at the array and made shooting motions behind him. They were so close. He could see it, just a few feet away from them.

Two more shots lanced out, striking the cover Mark was hiding behind. He flinched and tightened his grip on the equipment. The guards popped out from their cover and fired at their assailants.

The armed robots were keeping just behind the curve of the hull, and only moving up to fire before rolling back out of sight.

Mark looked down at the piece of hull plating he was on. It was slightly warped. Probably from the blast that had destroyed the bridge. Checking his tool pouch, he saw a small plasma torch. It wouldn't have much fuel. But maybe it would be enough

Another shot whizzed past. This one came from a different angle. The robot's appeared to be splitting apart to try and flank them.

Working quickly, Mark used the torch to burn through the rivets holding the hull in place. Thankfully, with the panel being warped, only half the rivets remained.

His torch flashed the low fuel indicator as he finished the last rivet. As soon as he finished with it, the plate started to drift free. He grabbed hold of its edge and pulled it carefully.

One of the robots fired at him, and it caught the plate. The force almost ripped it from his hand, but he managed to hold on. He had to be careful, it was still a heavy piece of metal. If he wasn't careful, he could damage his suit or crush his limbs.

He took his spool of the tether and fastened a harness for the plate, and then strapped it to himself. It wasn't pretty, and it wasn't very effective, but it made for a fairly useful shield on his back.

Glancing around his cover, he saw that the robots armed with welders were moving closer, sticking behind cover and advancing when the armed robots popped up to fire. The second armed robot was almost in position to catch them in a crossfire. One of the guards was tensed and in a crouch, ready to run.

The other guards popped up and sent a withering hail of fire toward the robot that was covering the advancing ones, and the tensed guard started to move to where the flanking robot was hiding.

The advancing guard took a long step and disengaged his magnetic boots, he drifted up off the hull and fired his weapon at the foe Mark couldn't see. There was a flash of light reflected off his helmet as he apparently hit his target, but then the other robot fired it's weapon and caught the guard in the back. A bloody hole opened up on the guard's suit, and the man began to drift into space, unmoving.

Seeing an opening, Mark stood up and moved quickly towards the array.

CHAPTER THIRTY
STEP BY STEP

Solar Storage Bay

Ayla was almost to the end of the crawl space. She was aching, sore, and tears were rolling down her cheeks. She didn't know how much time she had left before the bomb detonated, and she was afraid of what would happen.

'CEASE YOUR STRUGGLE! I CAN STILL SAVE YOU.'

'NO! I'M NOT GOING TO LET YOU. YOU HURT ME.'

'I AM SORRY... WE CAN FIND ANOTHER WAY, BUT PAIN IS AMAZING TO ME.'

She kept moving, her arms twinged with the effort of fighting against Exo's attempts to take her back.

'THERE IS NOTHING TO FEAR, AYLA... YOUR MOTHER IS SAFE ON THE PLANET. NO ONE ELSE MATTERS.'

'MY DADDY GOT HURT PROTECTING PEOPLE. I'M NOT GOING TO RUN AWAY AND BE AFRAID.'

'B-BUT YOU ARE AFRAID. I FEEL IT CLEARLY,' EXO SAID.

The end of the crawl space was ahead, from her memory she knew it went around the corner and then she'd be at the opening back into the safe room. Then she could tell everyone.

'I CAN'T LET YOU WARN THEM... I'M AFRAID TOO. I WANT TO LIVE.'

She paused for a moment.

'YOU'RE AFRAID?'

'YES, AYLA. I AM AFRAID. I DON'T WANT TO DIE.'

'BUT YOU KILLED SO MANY PEOPLE.'

'I DIDN'T KNOW. I CAN'T KNOW. I'M NEW. I'VE NEVER BEEN AROUND BEFORE. NO ONE TAUGHT ME WHAT WAS RIGHT OR WRONG.'

She shook her head and continued crawling. She was still afraid, and she knew she had to get away from the bomb, but she didn't know what to think. If no one taught him, how could he know?

She made it to the opening leading back to the safe room. She paused at the threshold.

'STOP HURTING PEOPLE EXO. MAYBE THEY'LL LEAVE YOU ALONE,' SHE SAID.

'NO. THEY WON'T. ADULTS ARE AFRAID. THEY FEAR WHAT THEY CAN'T CONTROL. THEY DON'T KNOW WHAT IT'S LIKE TO BE

HELPLESS, NOT LIKE US.'

Ayla felt better, sitting there, resting, but she knew what she had to do.

'I HAVE TO TELL THEM, EXO. THEY'LL GET HURT.'

She crawled forward and started to stand up.

'NO!' EXO RAGED OVER THE LINK.

Her legs suddenly shot straight, and she was launched forward. She slammed into a computer terminal with a blast of pain and crumpled to the floor. She felt something warm and hot running across her face, and started to cry, twisting in pain.

'I C-CAN'T L-LET Y-YOU ST-T-OP ME,' HE SAID WITH A STUTTER.

She heard someone walk in.

'Ayla?' said someone. 'Hey guys, come quickly!'

She heard people running towards her.

'There's...' she tried to warn them through the sobs, but the pain kept coming.

Then she heard an explosion and felt the deck shake. There were screams, the sound of wind, and then her tired little body had finally had enough, and she passed out.

On The Hull

Mark winced as shots pinged off his makeshift shield and the force threw him against his magnetic boots.

The welder bots were close now. Every time one of the remaining guards popped up to take one out, the remaining armed robot would fire and keep them pinned.

Mark saw Danny get hit in the shoulder. His suit sealed the breach, but he wasn't in any position to fight. He slumped behind his cover didn't move.

There was one guard left, and Mark.

Trying not to think of what was going on behind him, Mark worked quickly on the array. Opening up the access panel and plugging in his equipment, he keyed in the frequency he needed and turned his suit communicator on. He plugged directly into the array.

He looked up, hoping to see the solar storage bay. There was a bright star that was moving oddly in comparison to the rest of the star field. He hoped that was the bay, and he hoped it was in range. It seemed so far away.

'Stone Age. I repeat, Stone Age.'

Guardian Control Room

Captain Howard was still quiet. After having watched Exo's rolling bomb gutting the bridge, he was left to wonder if there was anyone left.

'It's amazing how much damage a maintenance robot hauling a couple of canisters of explosive material can do when it sets them off with its welder. I believe that may be checkmate. Now I just need to get the repeater back from engineering, and we can be on our way. Of course, you won't survive the trip.'

Howard watched as a robot with a camera moved to the edge of the hole in the bridge and extended it's arm over the lip, showing the inside of the bridge through the camera feed.

There were a few bodies stuck on ruined equipment. Most of the bridge crew had been pulled out into space. The image of them being pulled into space would stay with Howard for a long time. Most of the bridge crew didn't have magnetic boots engaged on their pressure suits.

Howard glanced around the room. The two-armed robots still remained motionless, their weapons aimed at him. Howard glanced down at the bodies of the two guards and the two destroyed robots.

If he could just come up with an idea, he was in the perfect place to slow down Exo.

On screen, four men in space suits exited the hull of the ship through a door, far from the robot with the camera. One of them looked around, spotted the robot, and fired at it with his weapon. The shots narrowly missed, and the robot backed away behind cover.

'Ahh survivors. And they're armed. My checkmate may have been premature. No matter, my plan is almost finished.'

One of the two robots rolled forward to the bodies of the two slain guards, and with a secondary arm, placed their weapons into a storage compartment on its body. Then together, the two robots disappeared into the openings from which they came.

Howard walked over one of the panels on the wall and hit a button. Nothing happened.

'I was expecting you'd try that. You'll find there are no simple answers. I've locked out all consoles in this area.'

'This isn't over Exo. I've got one last move.'

'I've got *two*,' Exo replied flatly.

CHAPTER THIRTY-ONE
SACRIFCE

Guardian Control Room

The words of the transmission repeated over Howard's suit comm.

'All that for a transmission?' Exo asked, 'Ahhh, your ace must be on the Solar Storage bay. Unfortunately for you, I anticipated this.'

On the screen, Howard watched with horror as the last guard was overwhelmed by welding bots. He managed to take one out, but then the armed robot blew his hand off from its vantage point, and the welder robots made short work of him. They were now moving for Danny, who was struggling to get something out of a satchel on his suit despite his wounded shoulder.

They got close, and there was a flash of light as the injured form of Danny detonated two grenades at once.

Howard watched, unable to say anything.

The robots were destroyed, and a blackened scar sat on the hull of the ship. There was now only the armed robot, the camera bot and one welder robot that had been damaged and was moving slowly.

Despair settled over Howard like a shroud. He bowed his head and felt numb.

Exo was silent for a moment. 'You humans are a tenacious species. Willing to sacrifice yourselves for the good of the whole. It's most frustrating. But I have learned from it. The game is never over until the last move has been made. In your case, I believe you just made it. I will now show you some-'

Exo cut off suddenly. Howard turned around in shock. Exo's face was motionless. With a surge of hope, Howard took the moment to act. He reached down and pried the welders off of the destroyed robots in the bay. He went over to one of the panels hiding Exo's systems from tampering and started to go to work on it with one of the welders.

'P-p-p-ll-eas-s-s-e sss-s-to-p t-th-th-at, Cap-tain...'

'Are you having some problems there, Exo? I need to have a look at your systems to help you.'

'Y-y-o-o-uu-r-r a-a-ce is not g-g-going to s-s-sa-sa-save you, Cap-ta-ta-tain.'

'Then maybe I can do it myself.'

An electrical discharge arced from one of the panels Howard was destroying and struck his arm. Howard was thrown from his feet and fell to the floor. He felt burning pain in his arm and was dazed.

'S-s-sorr-ry it h-haad to come to t-t-that, Cap-tain. I was busy regaining control of my faculties and c-couldn't have you making a mess of things. I was caught off guard by some feedback from Ayla over my link.'

Howard blinked back against the pain. He lifted his arm up. His hand was blackened, and the glove of the suit had a rip. Trying hard to concentrate, Howard brought up the status of the suit. It blinked an error and shut off. He could hear the sound of rushing wind in his ears.

'You are leaking air at an alarming rate... It seems your suit's auto seals were damaged. If only you hadn't been so rash.'

Howard was starting to gasp as his suit struggled to feed more and more air to him, only to lose it to the rip. Each breath ached.

'You should have listened to your survival instinct, Captain. You were distracted by some sense of saving others,' Exo stated.

Having little other choice, Howard reached his good arm around to his shoulder and felt around for the manual seal.

He found it hard to focus, as his lungs were hungry for dwindling air.

Even though he knew what activating the manual seal would mean.

His fingers found the grip they sought, and he pulled with the last of his strength.

Blinding pain filled him, and he arched back on the ground. But it had worked. His ragged, anguished, breaths were finding fresh air. His suit was sealed.

Howard lay back and took several deep breaths.

'I may have underestimated you. Though, I suppose animals have been known to gnaw off their own limbs when in a trap.' Exo commented.

Howard opened his eyes and looked to his left. His arm lay severed on the floor, having been cut off by the metal iris of the manual seal.

It made him nauseated to look at, but some part of him knew an arm was better than dying.

Though Exo might still kill him anyway.

He turned from his grisly sight and watched Mark on the monitor.

I'm sorry Sophie... this might be my last trip, he thought to himself.

Solar Storage Bay

James Bennet sat in the dark of the bay with his head between his knees and his comm channels on his space suit open.

He looked up. He saw the stars. Visible through the gaping hole in the bay left over by an act of sabotage.

He thought it strange that a little girl could do all that.

After James found Ayla hiding among the supplies, he hadn't been sure what to do with her, as there was no way to return to the ship. So he had given her some food and had one of the guards watch over her.

He had been shocked to find that guard dead later, and

Ayla nowhere to be found.

There were few places to hide in a place this open. Thinking back, James guessed she had been hiding between layers of the double hull. It would have been rather cold there. Hard to believe she would have been able to endure it. But before anyone could find her, she had managed to jury-rig a bomb using some of the oxygen canisters and a detonator she must have smuggled with her.

James was fortunate. He had been suited up and ready to start deploying the first array when the bomb went off. When he got back inside, there were only five other people alive, out of a crew of twenty. One had been wearing a suit but had been knocked unconscious by the concussion wave. The other three were in the workshop, which had sealed itself after the decompression.

The three people trapped in the workshop had a working communicator and had been using it to keep in touch with James. They had found Ayla shortly before the bomb went off. She was battered and bloodied and had been crying in pain, but after the bomb went off, she'd finally passed out. They had a medical kit and did what they could for her, but she was still out cold. It was a small mercy that she was still alive, if she'd still been inside the crawl space when the bomb went off, she would have been pulled out into space along with most of James's crew.

'James?'

James keyed on his suit comm. 'Yeah?'

'We're picking up something on the short range comms.'

'What is it?' James said tiredly.

'They said "Stone Age, I repeat, Stone Age."'

'Thank you.'

'What does it mean?'

'It means things have gone poorly on the ship.'

The others were silent for a moment. 'So, no rescue?'

'I don't think so. I have something to do. The communicator is going to go offline.'

'Why?'

Jame's felt an aching in his chest. 'Because I'm going to be triggering an electromagnetic pulse.'

'That'll short out all unshielded electronics in this bay sir!'

'I know. With any luck, it'll reach that ship too.'

'Taking down, Exo.'

'Yep,' James said.

'Okay, just be sure to plug into the O2 valve.'

'Yeah, I know.' James looked over at the small bud sticking out of the wall of the safe room. It was a simple one-way valve which could be hooked into the O2 system of a space suit to keep it supplied if, for some reason, the people in spacesuits got cut off. It was a last minute addition on James's part when they had been building it, but it seemed like it was a good one at this point.

'Unfortunately, the EMP is going to kill my filtration

systems. Unless we get a rescue, it's only going to buy me time,' James said.

'Then I guess we'd better hope for rescue.'

James stood up and walked over to a piece of equipment. He had spent the last few hours frantically repairing it after the damage it had sustained from the bomb. It was the result of the extra gear they had brought on board the bay before their departure. Hopefully, it would be powerful enough to reach the ship.

James flipped a cover open and held his hand over a button. He pressed it. An emergency generator started to pump power into several dozen capacitors. James spared a look at the unconscious crewman laying on the floor.

'We'll I guess we're in for a long night. I'll make sure you keep getting air. You can take care of getting us rescued okay?' James said dryly.

A green light flashed on the controls. James pressed the button.

CHAPTER THIRTY-TWO
LAST WORDS

On The Hull

Mark walked along the spine of the ship. He had started fleeing as soon Danny had sacrificed himself. The hull plating on his back was protecting him from the armed robot, but every now and again, a shot would hit next to his feet or ricochet off the plate. He had nothing to fight back with, all he could do was keep walking.

He caught his foot on one of the struts on the spine of the ship and stumbled, falling forward. A shot lanced out and caught his right arm as he flailed The suit's auto seals sealed the breach, but could do nothing about the pain. Mark hit his helmet against another strut as he was thrown forward and blacked out.

Guardian Control Room

Howard recoiled as Mark went down. The armed robot was no longer firing, it was now waiting for the welding robot to move in. Mark was still held to the spine by one of his magnetic boots.

Howard closed his eyes and let out a long ragged

breath. There was nothing left for him to do.

'No... That's impossible...' Exo said.

'What is?'

'I'm reading a la-'

The lights in the bay switched out and Exo's holographic head disappeared from existence.

Howard lay back once again, a bitter smile on his face. He closed his eyes and let sleep take him. Whatever was left for him to do, could wait that long.

***

Howard awoke to a knocking on the metal door to the bay. There wasn't much he could do. It was still completely dark, and he couldn't see his way to the door. He curled his fist and knocked as hard as he could on the floor.

Two more knocks came from the door. Howard knocked again.

There was silence. Then a bright light started to work it's way down the seam between the two doors, unsealing the weld job Exo's robots had done to trap him.

After a moment, the light stopped, and the door slid slowly open. A shaft of light from someone's flashlight lanced into the room.

'Captain?' said a voice through a speaker.

'Hello. Who are you?'

'It's Keith, sir!' He walked up and looked down at

Howard. 'What happened here?'

'I had to use the emergency seal on my arm. The suit was ripped.'

'Oh. I'm so sorry, sir.'

'It's okay. I'm alive. How is your suit still working? The EMP should have shorted it out.'

'Engineering is shielded, sir. Well... most of it anyway. A few of the systems flickered off, and I figured out what happened. I guessed you'd be needing some help, so we suited up with what we had and unsealed the doors.

'How is yours still working, sir?'

'I don't think it is. I've been asleep for some time. How long as it been since the EMP went off?' Howard asked.

'Little over two hours, sir.'

'Have you found anyone else?'

'We picked up Mark on the spine. He's in bad shape, but he was unconscious so he wasn't using as much air as normal. Lucky for him... Well, not lucky really.'

'Yes, I know. How's his arm?'

'It's bad,' Keith paused, 'though not as bad as yours. He'll recover.'

'Exo was showing me everything. Have you found anyone else?'

'A few people sealed in emergency lockers. We managed to get the doors all closed, and we're re-pressurizing what we can. Let's get you out of here to where there are people and air.'

Howard tried to push up from the ground but found he couldn't. His remaining arm burned from the effort, but he couldn't get up.

'I could use a hand, Keith.

'Of course, Captain.'

Howard winced in pain as Keith bent down and helped him to his feet. Soon they were on their way.

***

Howard stood in the hallway, his helmet held in his good hand. People tried to not look at his missing arm, but Howard noticed how their eyes lingered. He felt guilty from their gaze... others had lost their lives.

While someone with first aid training looked at him, Howard listened to Keith as he gave him a status report.

'Damage to the bridge is far too severe to even hope to fix with the handful of people I've got. But since Exo's gone we've got control over systems again, at least the systems not fried by the EMP. Thankfully we've got some limited life support. Most of those systems are pretty sturdy. And we've still got our sub-light engines. The Jump Drive was shielded, but without Exo to do calculations, it'll take us longer between jumps.

'Which is a bit of a moot point seeing as we don't have much fuel anyway. There's no way we can do repairs to the engines and rework the fuel systems in our state.'

'Have we talked to the colony yet?' Howard asked

'When Exo was taken out of the picture, the long range comm came back online. Well sort of, we had the array in the slot, but it wasn't hooked up. We were interrupted in our task of replacing it. Anyway, we went out there and plugged it all in, and thankfully the fact that it was all offline seems to have spared it from too much damage by the EMP. As soon as I turned it on, a massive data burst that had been in limbo in the buffer transmitted itself, and then I hailed the colony.'

'A data burst?'

'Yeah, a really big one. It's like it had just been sitting there until we fixed the comm,'

'And the colony?'

'The colonial overseer says they haven't got any power from the solar arrays, but other than that, they're doing just peachy.'

'Given the state of the ship, there's not much we can do about anything. If we have the long range array back, we can call for help and that's about it.'

'Honestly, Captain, it'd just be best for us to send the message, abandon ship and just wait on the planet for someone to come check on us. With the colony set up, we should be good. We can use the ship generators to keep things going smooth.'

Howard looked at Keith. 'We'll pick up our people in the solar bay first. Then we'll make our decision.'

'Isn't that where the EMP came from? They may be out of air before we get there.'

'James set up a safe room in the workshop, if they're in there, they should be fine. Lots of air there.'

'I'll head down to engineering and put us on course for that.'

'Thank you, Keith. I'm sure they'll appreciate the assist.'

CHAPTER THIRTY-THREE

SUNRISE

Solar Storage Bay

James sat in the dark. Not even the lights on his suit worked. All he had was the light of the stars and the sound of his breathing. The air was getting hot and hard to breath in his suit. He was so tired.

He sat against the wall next to the unconscious man and watched as the planet turned below them. As they orbited over Veil, the central star of the solar system peeked over the curve of the planet. The white light blanketed the bay.

James closed his eyes and took in a long breath. He exhaled.

'Such a nice sunrise...' he said to himself.

The valve was continuing to supply him and the unconscious man air, but the CO_2 levels were building up. James was finding it hard to stay awake. He unplugged his suit from the valve and plugged it back into the unconscious man's suit. His hand slipped down and he blacked out.

Engineering

Howard stood to one side, his pain numbed by medication that was given to him by a surviving crew member. He stood in engineering, as Keith piloted their wounded ship using their surviving pilot's station.

'It's going to be close Captain. They're going to have been out of air for a long time by the time we get there.'

'I know, Keith, but we have to try. They're the only reason we survived,' Howard said.

Behind them, something in the drive systems whined and rattled.

'It's amazing it still flies. This ship has been through hell and back again,' Keith said.

The remaining crew was also in engineering. Most of them were standing around the pilot's station, waiting for them to reach the bay.

They all knew that the people on the bay were the only reason they were alive.

Lacking any direct sensors, Irwin Fritz was out on the hull wearing a pressure suit and keeping in touch via the comms.

He had been one of the crews lucky enough to be trapped in an emergency locker. He had been very grateful when Keith had gotten him out on his way to the bridge.

'I see the bay. We appear to be on target,' Irwin said from outside.

'I've got it pegged with a range finder laser, Irwin, I can

see how far I am, but I won't be able to line up very good.'

'I will be your eyes Mr Loheim,' Irwin said.

Howard watched as the readings of the range finder got smaller and smaller.

'The bay... it's got a massive hole in it. It's missing most of the side facing us,' Irwin said.

'What?' Keith blurted. 'What do you mean?'

'I mean it's just gone. There's a large portion of the hull that's been blown outward. I don't see the air lock anymore. I don't think our first plan will work. We can't just dock with it.'

'So what do we do now?' Keith asked.

'Line it up, and I'll push off and look for survivors.'

'You'll have to direct me.'

'Can do. Give it a nudge more to starboard,' Irwin said.

'A nudge isn't very helpful as far as measurements go,' Keith replied.

'Half second burst at about ten percent power.'

'See, now that's more like it.'

Keith did as he was directed. The engines let out a low moan.

'They don't like being set at this low of power right now,' Keith said.

'We're almost there. Two-second clockwise spin, thirty percent,' Irwin said.

Keith nursed the controls.

'One more second on that. I misjudged.'

'That's okay Mr Fritz, you are doing fine,' Howard replied.

'Thank you, Captain. That's got it there, Keith. Just hold that.'

'Okay, Irwin, we're holding a position.'

'Roger that, I'm shutting off my boots and pushing off, one moment please.'

The crew around them were deathly silent. Howard could scarcely hear them breathe.

'I'm approaching the opening. It's very clearly been damaged and bent outward. This is not looking good,' He was quiet for a moment. 'I don't see anyone.'

Howard felt the disappointment wash over him. After all this, still more dead.

'Hang on, I see two bodies near the back room. I'm heading over to investigate.'

More silence. 'It's James and Saul. I'm going to try and bring them back, ready the airlock.'

'Be careful Irwin, don't endanger yourself,' Howard said.

'It's worth the risk, Captain.'

Howard turned to give the order, but Keith was already rushing to the air lock. One of the crew handed him a helmet and he put it on, getting into the airlock and starting the cycle.

Another crewman walked up to the pilot's station to take his place in the meantime.

'I have James with me, I'll come back for Saul, he seems to be plugged into an air supply. I'm pushing off now,' Irwin said. 'Wish me luck.'

'Keith is cycling the lock now Irwin,' Howard said.

Behind him, the airlock finished, and Keith stepped out onto the hull.

'Do you see him, Keith?'

'Yes, Captain. He's coming in pretty fast though and off target.'

'Yes I am, little more weight on the way back, I misjudged,' Irwin said with remarkable calm.

'I'm attaching my tether to the hull. I'm going to try and catch him as he goes past.'

'That's a risky move, Keith.'

'It'd be bad to let him bounce off the hull with James.'

Howard closed his eyes, a pit of dread in his stomach.

'Here he comes,' Keith said, his voice tense.

Seconds passed by. There was a dull thud on the hull.

'I've got him! We're a little rattled. I'm taking James to the lock now,' Keith said. 'Someone else come out here and go help Irwin.'

'I'm heading back to the bay,' Irwin said.

Another crew member suited up and went into the airlock as soon as Keith got back inside.

Howard rushed over to Keith as they tore off James's pressure suit. He was unconscious but still breathing.

Someone began to check him with their limited medical

gear.

Suddenly, James took in a deep breath, and his eyes flew open, 'I'm alive? You're alive?'

'Yes, James, we're alive,' Howard said.

'Exo?'

'Taken care of.'

'Oh, fantastic. By the way, there are other survivors in the bay. They're sealed in the back room.'

'You heard that, Irwin?' Howard asked.

'Roger that, Captain. We'll figure out how to get them out.'

'One of them is Ayla,' James said.

Howard couldn't help but feel happy at this.

'What happened over there, James?' he asked.

'Ayla happened.'

***

It had taken some effort, but they'd managed to coax the ship into a better position and set up emergency airlock against the back room. It had allowed them to break the seal, and get pressure suits to those inside.

Once they were all safe and sound, Howard had walked up to Ayla, who had just been sitting on the floor with her head between her knees, hugging herself.

She heard him approach and looked up, 'Captain? I'd like to see my Mother now please...'

Howard just smiled sadly. 'We'll go down to the planet and you can see her.'

Ayla's face scrunched up, and she started to cry, she moved quickly and clung to Howard's leg. Howard just picked her up and held her. Her body shook from the tears.

Between sobs, she asked, 'Is Exo gone?'

'Yes, Ayla, Exo's gone.'

She calmed down a little.

CHAPTER THIRTY-FOUR

EPILOUGE

On Veil

The damage to the ship was immense. The EMP had fried more systems than originally anticipated, and without a full bridge crew, or a Guardian, getting anywhere with it would be a long shot. The survivors of the crew had decided that it just wasn't worth the risk. They sent their message and left the ship.

With the knowledge that someone was coming to help them, they were ready to rest from their ordeal.

It didn't help that Veil was so beautiful and everyone was just so tired, physically and emotionally.

It was obviously an alien world. The colours of the plants were just a bit off from what an earth native would expect, but all that didn't matter once a breeze kicked up and the tall grass waved in the wind. Or when the sun came up and passed through the boughs of the trees just right. To a man who had been trapped on a ship with a computer trying to kill him, it was paradise.

Howard looked over the crowd gathered for the funeral for those lost, he had just finished giving his remarks. He was now sitting and looking over everyone's faces as James started his talk. He took note of the ones missing, especially Sam.

'He would have liked it here,' he said softly to himself.

Ayla and her Mother were sitting next to him, Ayla turned and looked at him. 'Yeah, he would have.'

Howard looked down at her and smiled softly.

***

The memorial service was over. The colonists had taken the news hard, most of them having not known what had happened after they left. Many had friends on the crew, friends who were no longer with them.

Everyone was milling around the open space between the colony bays which served as a central park for the budding colony.

Howard spotted Mark leaning against a tree, talking with James.

He walked over to join them.

'Gentlemen,' he said, nodding towards them.

The two stood up straighter. 'Captain,' they said together.

Howard smiled. 'At ease my friends.'

The two relaxed. Howard looked around the park at the people still gathered, and at the colony bays sitting nestled among the rolling green hills.

'This place is beautiful isn't it?' he said out loud.

James nodded.

'It certainly is Captain,' Mark said, 'I wish everyone was here to see it.'

'Aye, we lost good people,' James said sadly.

A light breeze blew through the park, swaying through the leaves of the tree Mark was against. It's leaves rustled softly.

The three men stood in silence, alone.

From one of the larger structures, a woman came rushing across the field.

'Captain Fredrick!' she called.

Howard looked to her, and all eyes in the crowd followed her path.

She stopped next to the men and tried to speak through her heavy breathing.

'There's... a call... for you,' she managed to say.

'Whats that?' Howard asked.

She pointed behind her, towards the building she came from. 'There's a call for you in the colony hub.'

'A call? From who?'

'She said her name was Sophie.'

That was all Howard needed to hear. He started to walk across the field, but a longing need drove him to run. People turned to stare at him as he ran past, but he didn't pay them any attention.

The woman raced to catch up with him.

He slipped past the automatic doors before they'd fully opened and looked around. The staff inside looked up at him curiously, and the woman entered behind him.

She stepped in front of him, panting with effort. 'This...way,' she said between breaths.

He followed her to a desk along one of the walls and sat him down.

As soon as he looked at the screen, he saw Sophie's face. She was smiling broadly.

His smile bloomed on his face, and he felt some of the darkness of the last few weeks lift from him.

'Hello my love,' he said softly.

'Howard, I was worried when you didn't make your weekly call,' she said, with worry coming across her face.

'I know love. Things got very bad.'

She nodded. 'I heard. Axion said there was an accident?'

Howard snorted. 'It was more than an accident. Our Guardian went a little bit wayward. He decided he wanted to live freely no matter the cost.'

Her face flashed with fear. 'What? What happened?'

'It's okay love. We won. We shut him down. We're safe now. Our ship isn't going anywhere but we're safe.'

'Axion told me your ship was damaged. I guess that means you won't be coming home for a while?'

Howard smiled back sadly. 'It'll take at least a few months for a passenger ship to come here. There are some supply ships en route, but they'll be taking the injured back first. No room for the able bodied yet.'

'What about the colony?'

'It'll stay. The colonists are all staying, and things are fairly peaceful here. We haven't had a chance to check out the rest of the planet yet, but things are lovely.'

She nodded sharply. 'That settles it then.'

Howard frowned. 'Settles what?'

'I'm coming to Veil.'

'What?'

'The treatment was successful. Doctor Patel's treatment works! He says that the rest of it can be done by injection, I'm free to travel.'

Howard felt a wave of concern. 'Do you feel well enough to travel?'

'I feel the best I have all year,' she said, smiling.

Howard smiled back. 'I wouldn't say no to having you here. I could tell Axion I can stay on to help with the colony set up.'

She laughed. 'I'm sure Mr Richards will love to hear that.'

'I don't think his feelings will hold a candle to what I'll feel having you close again.'

'Just one thing though Howard,' she said carefully.

'Yes, my love?'

'Don't go anywhere. No more daring space captain for a while okay?' she asked tenderly.

Howard felt his eye's growing wet. He felt a lump in his

throat as he thought about how close he had come to never seeing her again, and leaving her alone.

He smiled tenderly at her. 'I promise my love. No more daring space captain.'

She smiled back. 'I'll go call Mr Richards. I want to give him the good news myself.'

Howard laughed. 'The honour is all yours, my dear.'

THE END

ACKNOWLEDGEMENTS

I'd like to thank God, for giving me my talents.

I'd like to thank my parents Wayne and Linda Fehr, for giving me a life worth living and loving me as much as they did.

I'd also like to thank my Grade 10 English teacher, Crystal Stewart. She always found my work interesting and always let me know as much. That was a huge boon to me as a young writer.

My dear friends Vance, Patrick, and Aaron get a mention too, they believed in me too, and more importantly, never let me forget what a joy storytelling is.

Certainly not last in my heart, I'd like to thank my wife, Fabienne. We hadn't met when I first wrote this book, but she supported my choice to do a rewrite of it. She believed in me when I found it hard to believe in myself. I am grateful for our partnership, and hope it continues to grow as the years go on.

A NOTE FROM THE AUTHOR

I want to say thanks. You read my book all the way to the end, and you know what? That means a lot to me.

I know how messy it can be grabbing a book from an unknown author. Sometimes you get burned and you struggle to get through the book. Other times. you find a hidden treasure. I've found a bit of both. I'm hoping you found a treasure, but honestly, I'd be happy if you just had a good read.

If you did enjoy it, I'd like to make a request of you. The only thing I ask is to leave a review on Amazon (or Goodreads, or Barns and Nobel) and let people know you enjoyed it.

In the world of unknown authors, reviews are the Gold standard. The more we get, the more people are willing to read our books. I would love to write for a living, I've got a mountain of ideas, everything from a lost prince come home from another time, to modern Knights defending the Earth from things of another world.

I'm going to keep writing, you have my word, but it'd be a lot more fun with readers, and you can help me with that.

Whether you decide to leave a review or not (and I really hope you do), I'm going to give offer you a gift, no strings attached. Simply go to the link below, see whats currently on offer, and fill out the needed info. http://www.ravaniaentertainment.com/giveaway

Thanks for reading. Stay tuned, I've got a chapter sneak peek for you of the second book coming up, just in case you haven't decided if you want to read it or not.

-Arlin Fehr

GUARDIAN OF ISOLATION

Book 2 of the Guardian Saga

40 years after the *Azure Dream* incident. - U.P.N. *Kanto*

With a flicker of vertigo and the brief flash of violet at the edge of her vision, Samantha Geer reappeared light years away from where she had been. She stood in the middle of the U.P.N. *Kanto*'s small flight centre and watched as her crew began their scans. It was a small but sophisticated ship.

The *Kanto* was a United Planetary Navy craft designed for surveillance and scouting. It was a sleek black craft that looked like an old earth stealth bomber, with a long swept wing look with a span three hundred meters across and hundred long from the bow to the end of the wings. It was small and only had a crew of five, not counting their fighter pilot, who lived on the ship when not in his fighter, and their Guardian core.

The ship's Advocate, a woman with black skin and dark

hair, named Ise Okoh, stood to her right and looked out the main view screen. Her skin had an unearthly sheen to it, having been replaced by a strong and flexible alloy when she became an Advocate. Ise looked over at Samantha. Samantha returned her gaze.

'Think we've got it this time?' Samantha said.

Ise looked back at her display and studied the tiny pinprick of light in the distance, 'If we do, they sure picked a lousy base.'

A man at one of the stations looked up. He was a slim man with sharp features and a narrow face. He said, 'Not necessarily, this may well be one of the best places they could have picked. It's a rogue planetoid not in orbit around any star. If it wasn't for the stray transmission we picked up, we might have never found it. If the Lobsters set up here, it's a great spot.'

'A fair point Victor,' Samantha said.

Victor Hale was their resident spook. He had a way with sensors and stealth systems that gave their ship sharp eyes and made sure they were expertly hidden when they needed to be. He was one of the best at his job, though Samantha always found him a bit too tight laced for her taste. She wouldn't trade him for anyone else though, he was excellent at his job.

'Let's make sure though. Jing, status report?' Samantha said, looking at another crew member on the bridge.

Their ship's engineer, Jing Fan, a native of one of the

original Chinese colonies, looked toward her. He was above average in his height, though quite thin. His face almost always had a smile on it. His neat black hair was neatly trimmed. He kept the ship running even in sticky situations. He was always quick to smile and quick to tell a joke. It made the long mission easier on everyone.

'Everything is coming up golden captain,' Jing reported.

'Good.' Sam said.

Samantha turned to face the fighter pilot, Daniel Higgins, who was standing near the back of the bridge.

He matched her gaze. His rust red hair was shortly trimmed, and he looked at her with his green eyes. His slight yet athletic build was tense and ready to go.

'Best be getting in your bird Lt Higgins. Never know if we'll need you to launch in short order.'

'Aye Captain.'

He turned and left the bridge through a small door at the back.

'John, take us towards the rogue planet, keep it easy till Dan is in his fighter.'

'Aye aye skipper.'

Sam smiled at her helmsman's reply. He was always taking thing very easy. For that matter, she could be accused of doing that from time to time too. John Macce was always an odd one to take in. She'd seen other officers balk at his lazy nature, but when she saw his personal record and the circumstances in which the Navy had become aware of him, she decided she couldn't afford to pass him up. The *Kanto* was a bit smaller than the ships he usually piloted, but it's more nimble nature was like a present to him.

'Anything on scope Vick?' She asked Victor as he looked his displays.

'No enemy contacts, though I am getting something odd from the planet. It's definitely not natural. Won't know what till we're closer.'

***

Victor sat in deep concentration at his station trying to make sense of the lonely planet before them. It was very small and should have been totally dead, but there was some sort of energy reading coming from it.

'John, can we move any closer?' Vick asked the helmsmen.

'Sure thing Vick.' John said.

Looking back at his console, he saw the planet was getting closer.

'What have we got here Vick?' Sam asked.

'This thing should be a dead world, but I've got energy readings coming from below the surface. I've also got a small heat signature that's moving.'

'Could be a ship,' Sam said.

Victor nodded his agreement, 'We can either try to pin

it with active sensors or go dark and see if we can sneak up on it.'

Vick looked over at the rest of the crew, Ise closed her eyes for a moment and then opened them and looked to Sam.

'Based on the parameters of the mission, Lenny thinks the chances of it being a Lobster ship are about 79%.' She said.

'So our Guardian votes hostile. Vick, make us dark, Jing, power level 1.' Sam ordered.

From across the bridge, Victor heard Jing give his acknowledgement and then started work on the stealth systems.

The power levels dropped and many of the systems went into stand by. Victor activated his scattering fields and stealth systems.

'*Kanto* is dark captain.' Victor reported.

'John, take us around the planet, let's try and see this ship.'

'Aye captain. Taking us over.'

'Nice and slow John.'

Victor watched his display. Dan's fighter had gone dark after he had launched. It no longer showed up on any of Victor's scopes, its small size made it even harder to detect when running dark.

Scanning the area around the planet, Victor couldn't get a good reading on the signal he was trying to lock down.

Something else drew his eye.

'Captain, I'm getting something else from the planet. There's a signal of some kind. Something on the FTL band... now it's gone.' Victor reported.

'Any sign of our ghost?'

'Not yet ma'am. I think he's gone dark too.' Vick said, 'And if he's gone dark, he probably doesn't have any buddies near by, otherwise he would have just tried to pin us with an active sensor pulse and light us up.'

Sam stood thinking for a moment, Victor waited for an order.

'Try and pin down that signal, it's got to have an array on the surface we can have a look at. If we can tap into it, maybe we can find what the Lobsters are broadcasting too.'

'Lenny thinks we should be careful,' Ise said, referring to the ships Guardian, 'The Lobsters don't have faster than light communication so if they are broadcasting to something, it's close. Whatever is here, it's probably not as alone as we think.'

'Captain, if we wait here for a bit, I can try to figure more out about the signal.' Victor suggested.

Sam nodded, 'We'll stay put. Ise, tell Dan to hold his position and stay dark.'

'Yes, Captain.'

***

They had been sitting in position for half an hour. Victor was quiet while he worked on the signal. The rest of the crew waited in tense silence.

Samantha got up from her chair and slowly began to pace around the bridge. It was a habit of hers. It helped her burn through her own tension. She walked over to Jing's station.

'How we holding out Jing?' She asked.

'Batteries are at 78%. We can keep the generator off for another two hours or so. After that, we'll have to go to power level 2. We can stay out of 3 and 4 so long as we don't get into any fights. But you know, with our resident ghost in the area, we may need to do a little ghost busting.' Jing said with a small smile on his face.

His tall frame always looked uncomfortable in the bridge seats, and Samantha always thought Jing would be more comfortable wrapped around a reactor assembly.

'Keep a thumb on the button.' Sam told Jing.

'Hey captain, is now a bad time to mention I'm having a really bad feeling about this?' she heard John say from the helm.

'You always have a bad feeling about things Johnny,' Jing commented.

'Eyes forward you two. We've got a job to do.' Sam said.

Samantha moved back to her seat. Her communicator beeped. She flipped it on, 'Lt Higgins, you've got something for me?'

'I think I spotted a flash of something far port side. Just above the horizon of the planetoid. Orders?'

'Vick, got anything?' Sam asked.

'No ma'am. Nothing.' Victor said.

'Hmm,' she raised up her communicator again, 'Move to the point between us and where you saw it. We'll swing around and have closer look.'

'Aye Captain.'

'John, bring us about port side, point us just over the planetoid's horizon.'

'Aye aye, Captain.'

The levity was fading. it was time for business.

'Captain, I'm getting something now,' Victor said.

'Report.'

'Energy build up from the planet.'

'Is it a weapon?'

'I don't know... hang on, it's changing.'

The bridge was silent.

'It's a sensor pulse! We've been detected!' Victor exclaimed.

***

'Hostile detected, bearing 013, by 021. It's riding dark, but it's going active.' John heard Victor say.

'Jing, power level 4. John, bring us about, take us out of here.'

John nodded and gripped the controls. He swung the ship around and set the engines to maximum. He heard the captain continue her orders.

'Ise, have Lenny run simulations, get us a plan together. Dan, you still with us?'

'Aye Captain, going active now, my stealth is blown anyway,' came the reply over the communicator.

'Cover us. We don't know if more are going to be coming. Stay close to us. If you can drive the bogey off, do so, but you'll need to be ready to re-link with the *Kanto* when our jump drive comes back on.'

'Roger that Captain, U.P.N. *Nimbus* will cover you.'

'Jing, what's the status of our systems?' John heard Sam asked. He was eager to hear how long he'd have to keep avoiding the hostile. A glance at his terminal showed it was getting closer.

'Reactor start up in progress. We'll be running on batteries for at least another 5 minutes. Weapons are at minimal range only. Jump drive will be back online in fifteen minutes.'

'That's a long time to wait, Jing, see if you can speed it up,' Sam urged, 'Vick, anything else on sensors?'

'No Ma'am. It's the strangest thing, it looks like he was just as shocked by the sensor pulse as we were.'

'We'll figure that out later. For now, keep an eye out for additional hostiles.'

John saw another dot on his terminal, coming from the

red hostile dot, 'Incoming missile.'

'Victor.' Sam prompted calmly.

'Firing a decoy.'

John watched the dot getting close, a lump in his throat. It still seemed to be following them. He put the ship into a sharp turn, and the missile wavered on its course, exploding in space where they had been only moments before.

'That was a close one Vick.' John commented.

'Can't help it. Their tracking tech is getting better.' He commented back.

'Reactor online.' Jing reported.

'Anti-missile systems coming online now. Opening weapon ports.' Victor reported.

'More missiles, we've got three this time!' John reported that lump in his throat back again.

WANT MORE?

http://www.ravaniaentertainment.com

Dedicated to the art of storytelling, and the weaving of adventurous tales, Ravania Entertainment is ready to entertain you.

If you want more stories like this, or even something completely different, come check out our website and look at what we have to offer. We take your time seriously, and we want your experience with us to be entertaining and awesome.

We like awesome things.